Entice Me

ENTICE ME

by J. Kenner

Entice Me
Copyright © 2016 by Julie Kenner
Print Edition

Cover design: Covers by Rogenna

Published by Martini & Olive

From New York Times bestselling author J. Kenner comes a sensually seductive novella starring fan favorites Damien Stark and his wife, Nikki Fairchild.

Includes a special preview of Anchor Me, the highly anticipated fourth full-length novel featuring Nikki & Damien as they begin the next chapter in their life together.

I didn't understand passion until I met Damien, the man who turned my world upside down and swept me off my feet.

And though our life together feels perfect, we can't escape our secrets—and the danger that continually threatens to surface.

But for one night, I seek a respite. A birthday wish for my husband, my lover, my friend—one absolutely perfect night.

It is my most ardent wish.

And I only hope that it will come true…

Also by J. Kenner

The Stark Trilogy:
Release Me
Claim Me
Complete Me
Anchor Me

Stark Ever After:
Take Me
Have Me
Play My Game
Seduce Me
Unwrap Me
Deepest Kiss
Entice Me
Hold Me

Stark International

Steele Trilogy:
Say My Name
On My Knees
Under My Skin
Steal My Heart (short story)
Take My Dare (novella)

Jamie & Ryan Novellas:
Tame Me
Tempt Me

Dallas & Jane (S.I.N. Trilogy):
Dirtiest Secret
Hottest Mess
Sweetest Taboo

Most Wanted:
Wanted
Heated
Ignited

Also by Julie Kenner

The Protector (Superhero) Series:
The Cat's Fancy (prequel)
Aphrodite's Kiss
Aphrodite's Passion
Aphrodite's Secret
Aphrodite's Flame
Aphrodite's Embrace (novella)
Aphrodite's Delight (novella)

Demon Hunting Soccer Mom Series:
Carpe Demon
California Demon
Demons Are Forever
Deja Demon
The Demon You Know (short story)
Demon Ex Machina
Pax Demonica
Day of the Demons

The Dark Pleasures Series:
Caress of Darkness
Find Me In Darkness
Find Me In Pleasure
Find Me In Passion
Caress of Pleasure

The Blood Lily Chronicles:
Tainted
Torn
Turned

Chapter One

"**D**INNER AND A movie just isn't going to cut it," I say to Rachel Peters, my husband's executive assistant. We're on the fifty-seventh floor of Stark Tower, which is divided in half between the residence and the penthouse office suite. I'd been working in the apartment living room on my laptop while Damien took a phone call, but I'd slipped over to the office side specifically to enlist Rachel's help.

Her mouth twists, and she glances down at the print-out of Damien's agenda that shows both his personal and professional appointments. "Considering you're planning Mr. Stark's birthday, I'm going to assume that *movie* is a euphemism for something much more entertaining."

I roll my eyes. Yes, Rachel has become a good friend over the last few months. And, yes, I've become comfortable using corporate resources such as the limo without going through Damien. But that doesn't mean I think that having Rachel help me plan a night of unbridled sex with her boss would be a fair use of corporate resources. "Assume whatever you want," I say. "But what I need help pulling off doesn't involve *that* kind of entertainment." I bat my eyes innocently. "Believe me. I have the extracurricular part of the equation covered."

She presses her lips together in what I can only assume is an attempt to hold back a full-on laugh. "I bet you do," she finally says. "Okay, so just tell me what you need and I'll make it happen. But tell me fast. His car's going to be downstairs soon."

"We should have at least five more minutes," I say. "He was still packing his overnight bag when I left." Damien's flying to New York tonight, hitting a couple of meetings about Stark International's acquisition of a biomedical research facility in the morning, then returning to LA tomorrow just in time for cocktails with a tech genius he's been courting to head up a new division of Stark Applied Technology.

Damien had suggested that I join him on the trip, offering to reschedule the cocktails so that we could spend a long weekend in Manhattan. I turned him down, reminding him that I'm in the thick of putting together a key proposal for a corporate account.

That's not entirely a lie. I do have a corporate proposal on my desk. I've been working my tail off to build my web and mobile app development business, and if I win this new client, my clout in the industry will grow exponentially. So Damien knows I've been working almost non-stop on it.

What he doesn't know is that I'm taking a little break from it while I plan Damien's birthday extravaganza.

"A surprise party?" Rachel repeats when I tell her what I have in mind. "Are you sure?"

"You don't like it?"

"Are you kidding? I love it. I just don't see how you'll be able to keep it a secret. I mean, I have a few friends who wouldn't have a problem at all because their husbands are basically clueless. But Mr. Stark notices everything. And where you're concerned, he notices everything and then some. You really think you can do it?"

"Absolutely," I say, though I'm not sure at all, because the truth is, Rachel's right. But I want to do this. It feels right. And certainly more meaningful than a gift, because what the hell can you get a man who can buy anything he wants on a whim?

I tell Rachel as much, and she nods. "It's a good point. I mean, the man bought you an island, didn't he? It's kind of hard to top that."

"I did buy a really fancy watch that I had engraved, but that's just so *meh*. I'm going to put it in his Christmas stocking."

"It's a nice gift, though."

"I suppose. But what I want to give him is a celebration. Not just of his birthday, but of everything we have together."

When we'd said "I do," we'd both believed that we were setting out on the journey alone. After all, his father is a reprehensible man whom Damien disowned, and my mother is a controlling self-centered bitch whom I try to keep out of my head at all times. As far as we were concerned, our family consisted of exactly two people—me and Damien.

But nothing ever goes the way you expect it, and now Damien is close with Jackson Steele, the half-brother he never knew he had, and Jackson's wife Sylvia is not only Damien's former assistant, but has become one of my closest friends. They have two adorable kids, and Damien and I couldn't be happier spoiling our niece and nephew. In other words, in the blink of an eye, our family portrait went from two to six.

And if that wasn't enough, my father is now in the mix. I was a little dubious about his motives when he first stepped back into my life—and Damien was more so—but we've gotten to know each other over the last few months, and while I'm not sure I'll ever truly think of Frank as my father, he's definitely part of my family.

And of course we have our friends. Jamie and Ryan and Ollie and Evelyn and Blaine and Wyatt and Cass and Siobhan and Lisa and Preston and Rachel and on and on and on.

For a girl whose only family was once the mother she despised, I've grown into a woman surrounded by an extended, boisterous, loving family made up of relatives and friends—and I owe most of that to Damien.

So that's what I want to celebrate on his birthday—the family we've made together.

"I can't pull it off without your help," I tell Rachel.

"I'm not sure you can pull it off with my help," she counters. "His birthday is next Friday. In case you hadn't noticed, it's Thursday. That gives us just a little over a week to plan. That's hardly any time at all."

"No, this is good. Less time for him to see that we're up to something."

"I guess…"

"It'll work," I say firmly, as much to convince her as myself. "But I need you to keep his calendar clear and help me with some of the logistics."

She scrunches up her nose. "I'll do whatever you need, but honestly, Nikki, come on. We both know you're never going to manage to pull it off."

"Pull what off?" The surprising sound of Damien's voice makes me jump, and I fight the urge to cringe as I meet Rachel's apologetic eyes before I quickly turn around to face my husband.

He's just a few feet away, his overnight bag slung over his shoulder. He's dressed in jeans and a short-sleeved linen button down. It's a simple, casual look, but so damn compelling. I want to reach out and touch him. I want to feel his arms around me, his lips brushing mine. I want to get lost with him—and I can't help but wonder if there will ever be a time when I'll no longer have such a deep, sensual, visceral reaction to nothing more than the sight of him.

Mentally, I shake myself, then hurry toward him. "I thought you were still in the apartment." I slide my arms around his waist. "Is your car here already?"

"It is," he says, nodding at Rachel. "Tell Edward I'll be right down."

"Of course, Mr. Stark."

"I just want to hear what my wife is going to pull off before I go." The corner of his mouth twitches as he speaks, and I narrow my eyes at him. Of course, I'd thought I'd distracted him. And, of course, he hadn't been distracted at all.

"I was trying to convince Rachel to secretly reschedule your cocktails with Noah tomorrow for next week so that I could show up at the airport in your limo and, you know, take you out for an evening of dinner and debauchery." I lift a shoulder and give him a seductive smile. "But there's no point now that you know about it."

"And I told her she'd never pull it off anyway," Rachel adds. "Because first of all, if I rescheduled Noah, you might fire me, and that would totally suck. And second, surprising you takes a minor miracle." She waves her hand, indicating Damien standing right there, then looks at me. "I rest my case."

I sigh heavily. "Well, it was a worth a shot." I point a finger at Damien. "Just remember when you're having drinks with Noah what you could have been doing instead." I press my mouth to his, kissing him long and hard and so deep, I feel it all the way down to my toes.

When I pull away, I'm breathless. And though he's doing a damn good job of staying professional in front of Rachel, I see the banked heat in his eyes and the restraint in his body. He's like a spring—and right now he's held together by a single tight wire. Let it go, though, and he'll have me pressed against a wall and naked before I even have time to take a breath.

The thought makes me shiver—and makes me anticipate his return home all the more.

"Until tomorrow, Mrs. Stark," he says, clearly following my thoughts.

"I'll be waiting," I say, then watch as Rachel hands him an itinerary. He tucks it his briefcase, kisses me once more, then heads toward his private elevator.

I don't exhale until the doors close behind him, then I sag with relief and watch as Rachel does the same.

"I take it back," she says. "That was one hell of a good performance. You might just manage this after all."

"ARE YOU KIDDING?" Jamie says. "You're never going to pull that off. Rachel's insane. And frankly, I'm a little concerned about your mental health, too."

"Very funny," I say, as Lady Meow-Meow, Jamie's fluffy white cat, kneads my skirt with her claws and purrs as loud as a lawn mower. "Yes," I say, running my hand over her head, "I miss you, too."

We're in Jamie's condo, which hasn't changed that much since I used to live here with her. It's still decorated in Early American

Garage Sale, but she's added more movie posters to the wall.

My old bedroom is now an office, although when I was in there earlier, I noticed that she's stopped using the closet as a giant filing cabinet. Now, it holds a full wardrobe of men's clothes.

"So where's Ryan?" I ask, referring to Jamie's boyfriend, Ryan Hunter, who also happens to be the Security Chief for Stark International.

"Oh, he's at his place today."

I frown. "His place? I saw the closet and assumed he moved in with you."

She lifts a shoulder, then pulls her legs up under her, yoga-style. She's in the rattiest clothes she owns, isn't wearing a bit of make-up, and still manages to look glamorous enough she could be mistaken for an A-list star. "Well, he's here most of the time," she says, "but it's not a one-hundred percent thing. I mean, a girl needs her space, right?"

I shift on the sofa so that I can see her better, and in the process disturb Lady Meow-Meow, who nips the back of my hand, then hisses lazily before jumping down to the carpet. "Is something going on with you two? I mean, you're okay, right?"

"Of course we're okay. In case you missed the memo, I'm head over heels, one-hundred percent in love with Ryan."

"Actually, I got that memo." My best friend—who used to approach sex as if it was a hobby—is now devoted to just one man. Or, I'd been assuming she was. Now, though, I'm getting a weird vibe.

"James," I say, calling her by the familiar nickname. "What's going on?"

"Nothing. Really."

I cross my arms. "Tell."

She sighs heavily. "Honestly, Nicholas, it's no big deal. He just started up with the wedding talk and…" She trails off with a shrug.

"Really?" I couldn't be happier. "I've been wondering when I could go shopping for a matron of honor dress."

Jamie shakes her head violently. "No, no, no. That conversation is way off limits. I can love him without marrying him."

"Yeah, but—"

"No," she says adamantly. "Conversation over. Done. *Fini*. End of story."

"Fine." I hold up my hands, because I know better than to push. Despite the fact that her parents are amazing and have been happily, blissfully married for decades, Jamie reviles the institution of marriage. "Not yours," she once told me. "You and Damien were absolutely right to get married. It fits you perfectly. But me? Not so much."

I don't know why she feels that way, but I do know that I'm afraid for her and Ryan. She adores him, and he's mad for her. But if he pushes too hard, he may end up pushing her away.

And since I don't want to accidentally contribute to that possible rift, I back quickly and firmly away from the topic. "Just as well, because you and Ryan are *so* not my problem. I need to figure out where to have the party and how to keep it a secret."

"Like I already said, the secret's gonna take a miracle," Jamie says. "As for the location, I figured you were having it at your Malibu house. But you could have it at the apartment. He wouldn't expect a party in Stark Tower."

She has a point, but neither of the ideas thrill me. "I want something different. Something unexpected."

"The island?"

"We go to the resort all the time," I say, referring to The Resort at Cortez, a Stark Vacation project that's also all in the family considering Sylvia was the project manager and Jackson the architect.

"Not that island. I'm talking about the one out in the Caribbean. The island he bought you after your honeymoon."

"Oh!" I consider that. We'd been hounded by paparazzi on our honeymoon, and in order to get truly, completely, one-hundred percent away, Damien had bought a small island. As one does. If one happens to have billions of dollars tucked away, anyway.

"That would be great," I say, "except there's just a tiny house with only one bathroom. Somehow I don't think that's the kind of destination party our friends would appreciate."

"Are you saying we're all too prissy?"

"Pretty much."

"You got that right." She stretches her legs out so that they rest on the coffee table, then pats her lap, trying to urge the cat back up. No luck. "Sophistication and class, then. Okay. So, um, what about Starfire?"

It's not a bad suggestion—the Starfire Resort & Casino in Vegas—also a Stark property—is one of the most opulent hotels west of the Mississippi. But it's not really what I had in mind.

"Well, why not?" Jamie asks, when I tell her as much.

"One, it's Vegas. And Vegas just doesn't scream classy to me, even if the hotel itself is amazing. Two, we were there not that long ago. Three, I was thinking it would be a relaxing weekend with friends. Vegas is a loud, all-night kind of place."

"For some of us, loud and all-night *is* relaxing."

"Yes, but the only one of us that applies to is you."

Jamie pouts. "Are you saying Damien's birthday isn't all about me?"

I whack her with the pillow, and Lady Meow-Meow—who'd been considering leaping back up to the couch after all—lifts her tail straight up, turns around, and heads for the kitchen.

"Think," I order as I reach for my phone, which has just pinged with an incoming text.

I grab it, assuming it's Marge, the receptionist at my office suite.

It's not. It's Damien.

Miss you already. Dinner under the stars when I get home? I'll keep cocktails with Noah short. If I tell him you're waiting for me, I'm sure he'll understand.

I bite my lower lip, fighting an almost painfully broad smile.

When have I ever said no?

His response is almost immediate.

And I do so like that about you.

I laugh out loud, and Jamie, who's been watching me, shakes her head with mock disapproval.

"Get a room, you two."

I lift a brow as I type out another response. "That's kind of what I'm planning."

Looking forward to tomorrow night. And to the stars.

There's a brief pause, and then one final text.

Me, too. Until then, imagine me, touching you.

I sigh and look up at Jamie.

"Don't get all gooey on me. You're supposed to be focusing."

"I have a date," I say. "Dinner under the stars tomorrow night. I presume he means at home, but if he's going to take me out, all the better." Or not, I think. Because at home provides another level entirely of sensual possibilities.

"Where can you eat on the roof, anyway?" Jamie asks.

"Le Caquelon," I say, referring to our friend Alaine's restaurant. "Although we always eat in one of the private booths on the inside. When we first got together, Damien took me to the Pearl Hotel. We ate outside on the terrace."

That had been a magical day. At the time, I barely knew him, and I'd stormed to his office to chew him out about a work fiasco. He'd calmed me down and invited me to lunch. I'd expected a restaurant downtown. Instead, he'd flown me to Santa Barbara.

"Actually, what about that?" I say, my mind suddenly whirring.

"What about what?"

"Damien owns the Santa Barbara Pearl Hotel. And we could use the jet to ferry anyone there who doesn't want to drive."

"That's kind of a great idea."

"It is, isn't it?" I'm completely pleased with myself. "Now I just have to get it arranged with the hotel, invite everyone, figure out the decorations, and at least eight thousand other things I'm forgetting. All within a week. And keep Damien from clueing in." I frown at Jamie. "I can do it, right? Tell me I can do it."

"Oh, totally," she says dryly. "No problem at all."

Chapter Two

FRIDAY IS A complete waste of a work day—but I don't mind because I manage to make a ton of progress on the surprise party. And I don't care what Jamie and Rachel think, I am *so* going to pull this off.

Even though Damien was in New York most of the day—and is now *en route* from the airport to the Stark Century Hotel where he's meeting Noah for cocktails—I'd done most of my legwork from my office in Studio City. Just because there's less risk of Damien running across a stray scrap of paper.

I'd started the day with the guest list, methodically creating a spreadsheet with the name of everybody I want to invite, and then going one by one through the list and either calling or emailing them. Most responded right away, and so far I only have two regrets—my friend Ollie, because he's in Munich doing some sort of corporate legal work for a major client; and

Sylvia's brother Ethan because he's in Australia with a girl he met recently.

I still have a few more people to call, and some who haven't reported in, but it's shaping up to be a nice crowd.

I'd also spent over an hour on the phone arranging for decorations and the cake. Sally Love, the owner of Love Bites, did the cupcakes for our wedding reception, and she's agreed to not only create a massive cake for the party, but to also take care of transporting it to Santa Barbara. I'm leaving her to decide on design and flavor—she's the hottest celebrity dessert chef around these days, and I trust her completely. She's also a good friend, and I know she'll do us right.

As for the rest of the food, I was planning to have the hotel cater, but when I invited Damien's childhood friend Alaine Beauchene, he insisted on handling at least one station. Alaine is the owner of Le Caquelon, a popular fondue restaurant, and although I'd intended him to only come as a guest, I've had his fondue and it's amazing. So no way was I going to turn down that offer.

Unfortunately, by the time I had to leave the office to head to Stark Tower, I still hadn't touched base with Richard Layton, the manager of the Pearl. Instead, we've been playing phone tag all day. Which makes me nervous, considering the hotel accommodations are pretty much the cornerstone of my whole birthday scheme.

Now, I'm heading down the 101, hoping to get back to the apartment in record time.

Because tonight, I have a plan.

My phone rings, and I press the button on the steering wheel to connect the call.

"Mrs. Stark?"

"Call me Nikki, Edward," I say for the billionth time, even though we both know that as Damien's primary driver, he'll never back off the formality.

"Of course, Mrs. Stark."

I bite back a smile. "Where is he?"

"I just left him at the hotel. I told him I needed to get gas and asked when he wanted me back."

"Brilliant," I said. "How long's he planning on being with Noah?"

"Apparently Mr. Carter has plans later this evening. Mr. Stark told me to expect him to be ready to leave by six-thirty."

I glance at the clock and realize I need to hurry. "Okay, thanks. I'll be home in ten. I'll text you when I'm all set."

"I'll be in position," he says, and it's my turn to laugh. The way we're talking you'd think we were doing espionage.

No sooner have I hung up with Edward

than my phone rings again. This time it's Richard, and we're able to smooth the way through the hotel plans. Basically, I want the party to be in the Presidential Suite. It's an incredible suite with a marble staircase, a wall of windows that rises two stories with a view of the ocean, and a rooftop garden.

The hitch is that Damien always stays in that suite when we go to the Pearl. Which means we either have to lie and tell him it's occupied—which is risky as he might find out otherwise during the trip—or I have to come up with some clever way to get him out of the room so that the party guests, food, alcohol, and decorations can all move in and get set up.

"How long will that take?" I ask Richard, wincing a little even before he answers.

"An hour minimum."

"Could you pull it off in forty-five minutes?"

He makes a strangled, helpless sound. "For Mr. Stark, I think we can manage."

"You're amazing," I say, and then we turn to the next task—trying to figure out what the excuse to leave the room could possibly be.

"I'll keep working on it," I say as I turn into the Stark Tower parking garage. Nothing I've come up with is even remotely convincing or certain. A birthday dinner is logical, but dicey. Because first, I want Damien to be hungry for the spread of food at the party. And second, what if he decides that ordering room service and having dinner in bed is a more entertaining way to spend his birthday? If I disagreed, he'd know right away that something was up.

I frown, considering. Maybe theater tickets? Richard would probably like the extra time.

I make a mental note to see what's playing, and then park my car and hurry toward the elevator.

Less than fifteen minutes later, I've freshened my make-up and am wearing my favorite casual dress. I love it because it's made of soft jersey material and is incredibly comfortable. I chose it because it's easy to get on and off.

I text Edward, pack a tote with the few essential items I need to carry out my evening's plan, and then head back down into the parking structure.

The limo is waiting for me by the elevator alcove, and Edward comes over to open the door for me. "Good evening, Mrs. Stark."

"Thanks for doing this, Edward," I say.

"Now, you know it's no trouble. The more I'm driving, the further I get in my book."

"What are you listening to now?" Edward is addicted to audiobooks, and we've been comparing notes on the classics.

"*To Kill a Mockingbird*. Can you believe I've

never read that book before?"

"It's one of my favorites. I'm surprised you got through school without reading it."

He winks at me. "I managed to get through school without doing a lot of things. I regret some of them now. But not all," he adds, with a devious smile.

"I re-stocked the bar," he says as I slide in. "And everything else you asked for is stocked as well."

"Thank you."

"Would you like the privacy screen up on the way back to the hotel?"

"Please," I say. Often I keep it down when it's just Edward and me, but today I have a wardrobe change to take care of.

Traffic is light, but I work quickly, and by the time we're close to the hotel, I'm putting the finishing touches on my surprise.

"Are you ready, Mrs. Stark?" Edward asks over the intercom. "I can circle once if you need more time."

"I'm good," I assure him. "Do you see Damien?"

"He's just stepping out of the hotel. Have a lovely evening, Mrs. Stark."

"That's my plan," I reply as the limo pulls to a stop outside the hotel. I'm sitting on a rear-facing bench just in front of the privacy screen. There's also a black velvet curtain that bisects the limo just a few feet in front of me, and I've closed it. The result is that I'm in a small, secluded section with no view of the rest of the passenger area.

All I can do is wait, which I do impatiently until I hear the click of the handle and then the door being opened at the far end of the limo. I lean forward, then peek through the slit between the two halves of the curtain and watch as Damien enters and gets settled. He has his phone out, the bright screen illuminating his face as he taps something out. I bite my lower lip, hoping that I'm right about the message he's sending.

"Are you heading home, Mr. Stark?" Edward asks, and though it may be my imagination, I think I hear a note of amusement in his voice.

Damien nods as Edward shuts the door. A moment later, I hear a sharp *ping* from the storage area on the sidewall of the limo, just a few feet from Damien. I press my lips together, my heart starting to beat faster. *Yeah*, I think. *The game is on.*

I know I should move further back to ensure he doesn't see me, but I can't resist watching, and so I hold the curtain tightly shut and peer through the only gap that remains, barely larger than a pinhole.

I watch as Damien frowns, then slides

across the bench seat to the compartment designed as a holding place for small personal items that might otherwise roll across the floor or get misplaced in the usually dark interior.

I know of course what he'll find in the compartment: My phone. And a pair of lace thong panties.

He pulls out both, and even in the dim lighting I can see amusement in his eyes—along with a rising heat.

His gaze moves slowly around the limousine's interior, and I can almost see him running through the possibilities. Is Edward taking him to meet me? Or am I right there, just a few feet away?

He eases forward, crouching as he moves toward my end of the limo. I back away, careful not to move the curtain, and sit down, my arms casually thrown over the back of the bench, my legs crossed, and a sparkly high-heeled sandal dangling from one foot.

I see his fingers first as he reaches into the gap between the halves of the curtain. Then he pushes them apart in one quick, efficient movement that has the drapery rings clacking—and which reveals him on his knees in front of me.

"Ms. Fairchild," he says, as he looks me up and down. "This is a pleasant surprise."

"I'm very glad to hear it." I run my fingertips down my cleavage to the silk bodice of the gown I'm wearing. Except it's not a gown—it's actually a robe that's designed to look like an elegant garment. And it's held together by one simple tie around my waist.

"You said we'd have dinner under the stars," I say, shifting my legs so that part of the robe falls open to reveal my bare calf and part of my thigh. "I thought I'd facilitate that."

As I speak, I press the button on the nearby console that operates the sunroof. Above us, two large panels slide open, allowing in the cool night air, and revealing a blanket of stars. We're in the flats of Beverly Hills now, just starting to climb up toward Mulholland Drive. The ambient light of the city is softer here, and the absence of a moon allows the sky to twinkle above us, as if it's winking approval at my plan.

He inches forward, then places a hand on each of my knees and gently forces me to uncross my legs. As he does, he grazes my skin with his thumbs. I bite back a moan as the contact sends a wild electric current straight up my thigh to my already sensitive, swollen sex.

Even in the dim light, I can see the corner of Damien's mouth twitch, and am absolutely certain that he understands the effect he's had on me. More, I understand that no matter what

I'd planned for this evening, I'm no longer the one in charge. I am completely at his mercy, having surrendered everything when I melted at his touch.

"So," he says as he casually brushes a kiss on my inner thigh, just above my knee. "Dinner?"

"Y—yes." I have to struggle to get the word out because now he's sliding his hands along my legs, easing higher and higher with such leisurely progress that I fear I'm going to scream with frustration any moment now. "I, um, had Edward stock a selection of take-out in the buffet."

"Interesting," Damien says, glancing over his shoulder to the sidewall of the limo where there is a hidden buffet behind the bench that runs along that side of the vehicle. It's a match to the full bar that runs the opposite length.

He reaches for the sash at my waist and gives the bow one quick tug. Immediately, the robe falls open. Damien draws in a breath as his gaze skims over my naked body, from my sex, to my breasts, to my eyes.

And then—yes, oh god, yes—he slides his finger over my very wet, very sensitive labia, making me tremble with an unrelenting, demanding need that I feel through my entire body. The tightening of my breasts. The heaviness between my legs. The tingling of my lips. The warmth of my skin.

"Damien." His name is a plea, but he ignores it. Instead, he lifts his now slick finger to his lips, and so slowly it's almost painful, he sucks off the taste of me.

Then he looks at me with such desire it's a wonder I don't come right then.

"It's not food I'm hungry for, Nikki," he says as he gently spreads my legs. "It's ambrosia."

I whimper, as he slowly draws his tongue along my inner thigh, teasing and licking as he comes closer and closer to my center. So that when he's finally there—when he finally closes his mouth on my sex to suck and tease and lick—the sensation is so far beyond incredible that I'm not entirely sure how I'm going to survive.

But it's not just his mouth teasing me. With one hand, he presses against my inner thigh, his thumb grazing the soft skin between my leg and my sex. With the other, he reaches up to tease my breast, heavy and sensitive in his palm. Every part of me is on fire, and I grind against him, utterly lost, wanting more. Wanting absolutely everything.

I slide my hand up to my other breast, then mimic his touch as he pinches and squeezes my nipple so that threads of heat course through me like strings connecting every erogenous zone on my body.

His hand on my thigh shifts, and his finger teases my entrance even as his tongue flicks over my clit. I cry out, bucking up as he thrusts two fingers inside me, then sucks hard on my clit as I bite my lower lip and try to focus on breathing because I'm close—I'm so damn close—and every sensation is mixing together, building and building to what I am certain will be an explosion that rips me apart, satisfying me by completely destroying me.

"Yes," I hear myself saying. "God, Damien, yes. Just a little more. Just a little—"

But then his mouth is gone, and I feel the shock of cool air on my sex instead of his warm mouth. I open my eyes to see that he has moved away, his head now tilted up to my face, his eyes burning with sensual intensity as he looks at my fingers, so tight now on my breast.

"Did I say you could touch yourself?"

I swallow, my hips shifting shamelessly as I search for contact that isn't coming. "Damien, please."

"Did I say you could touch yourself?"

Slowly, I shake my head as a new kind of excitement builds inside me. "No, sir," I admit as I lower my hand. My whole body is suddenly hyperaware, on fire simply from the tone of his voice and the anticipation of what is to come.

"That's twice you've been naughty."

I frown, confused. "Twice?"

"I told you we'd dine under the stars. But since you took the liberty of making arrangements, now I'm going to have to cancel a reservation."

"Oh." I lick my lips as he reaches out a hand for me to take.

I do, and he gently kisses my fingertips before pointing to the area beneath the skylight and saying very firmly, "You want to be under the stars? There. On your knees. Elbows to the ground. Head down. Knees apart."

I comply, then tremble violently when he presses the palm of one hand to my ass, and slides his other hand up between my legs, stroking my exposed sex. "Beautiful," he murmurs as he thrusts his fingers deep inside me, then traces the rim of my anus with his thumb. "I like you this way, baby. Wide open for me. Ready. Do you know how wet you are?"

"Yes," I murmur, then squeal as his palm smacks my ass.

"Naughty, too," he says, then rubs the sting away with a gentle hand. "Can't have that, can we?"

"No, sir," I say, craving that sweet sting

again, then sucking in a breath when it comes, the impact followed by a lingering heat that settles inside me, making me even wetter. That delicious pain getting all twisted up with the arousal coursing through me, so that with each smack of his hand, I get more and more turned on, my cunt so sensitive and needy that I think I just might die if he doesn't hurry up and fuck me.

Thankfully, he doesn't make me wait. He strokes me, fingers dipping into my cunt and then stroking my perineum in a wild and crazy rhythm that has me whimpering and begging. And then, when I think I can't take it any more, I feel the press of his cock at my center as he grabs my hips with both hands. He starts out easy, but I can't wait, and I press back hard against him, impaling myself on him.

"Nikki! Oh, Christ, baby, yes."

"Please, Damien," I beg. "Please." I can't manage any more words, and he thrusts inside me, again and again, spinning us both further and further into space. Harder and faster until he's so close, and he reaches around to tease my clit and take me over with him, until we explode together, and then collapse on the floor of the limo, curled up together in a tangle of limbs.

For a moment, we lie there in total silence, just staring up at the stars that twinkle above us. Then Damien takes my hand and very sweetly lifts it to his lips and kisses my palm.

"I liked my surprise," he says. "And I think that was one of the best dinners I've ever had."

Chapter Three

IT'S EASY TO keep the secret from him on Saturday, too. We're home all day, just lazing around. During the day, we both tackle some of the work we've brought home, although I spend a lot of time not working on my proposal. Instead, whenever Damien isn't around, I open a new browser window and search out amazing gifts for his party. Not for Damien, but for gift bags.

Since the guests are all taking time out to travel to Santa Barbara, I want to make sure everyone has something nice to go home with. And, honestly, it's fun. Before life with Damien, the most I could offer party guests was a really kick-ass margarita, courtesy of my Texas roots.

Now, I can have a special thank you ready for each of them.

In the end, I come up with body lotion and custom bracelets for the women, shaving soap and designer cufflinks for the men, and tiny bottles of wine and scotch for everyone. The trick, of course, is that all the items have to be delivered by Friday so that I can put them together in the customized gift bags I also ordered. Then I'm going to pass it all off to Rachel, who's arranged to get everything delivered to the hotel by early Friday morning.

I even have special bags for Ronnie and Jeffery, despite the fact that Syl says that she's only going to let them stay long enough to yell "surprise" to Uncle Damien before Stella, their nanny, takes them back to their room.

What I still don't have is an actual gift for Damien. Yes, I told Rachel that the party is the gift, but I didn't really mean it. I may not adhere to most of my mother's rules of etiquette, but the Elizabeth Fairchild Birthday Party Guidelines definitely apply in this case: Thou shalt always give the guest of honor a thoughtful present to unwrap.

But what?

It's a question I'm still pondering on Sunday when we head over to the Pacific Palisades for an afternoon at Jackson and Sylvia's house.

"Sex toys," Jamie says, when I tell the girls my dilemma. We're drinking mimosas on the rooftop patio as the guys hang out on the lawn doing manly things with the grill and supervising Ronnie on the swingset.

"What?" Jamie asks as everyone turns to stare her. "I bet he'd totally appreciate an imaginative sex toy. I know Ryan did," she adds with a wink.

"But what could I buy him that he doesn't already own?" I keep my voice deadpan, which makes Jamie bark with laughter and Siobhan go bright red.

"You two are like a vaudeville act," Cass says, then leans over to Siobhan. "It's okay, sweetie, they don't bite hard."

"I'm not a prude," Siobhan protests. "Redheads just blush easier."

"She's a prude," Cass says in mock confidence. "Well, in public anyway. In private she's a wildcat." That earns her a shove from Siobhan, with whom she's sharing a two-person lounger. Siobhan is in a loose skirt and T-shirt because she burns easily, and Cass is decked out in tiny shorts and a bikini top that shows off the gorgeous tattoo of a brilliantly plumed bird covering her shoulder and trailing down her arm.

Earlier, I'd pointed out that technically it's winter, but Cass just shooed my words away. "What's the point of living in LA if you can't pretend like every day is summer?" Honestly, I really couldn't argue with that.

Cass is Syl's best friend, and she owns a local tattoo shop. Apparently, she's given Syl every one of her tats. Frankly, I'd been surprised when I learned that Sylvia had any tattoos at all. But that's the best part of this growing web of friends and family—I keep learning more about the people I love.

Right now, though, I'm close to disowning them all. "For the record, you guys are no help at all," I protest grumpily.

"I can go shopping with you this week," Jamie says.

"Great. For what?"

"Beats the hell out of me. But I figure if we combine the shopping with a few stops for wine along the way, sooner or later, something will seem like an amazing gift."

I roll my eyes, but I don't say no. It may not be the best plan for finding Damien's gift, but the afternoon will definitely be entertaining.

"You're throwing him a kickass party. Just leave it at that." Syl's been listening from a table in the shade, where she's been sitting with Jeffery, who's attacking a cup of yogurt with gusto. "I promise you Damien won't feel slighted."

"Fine." I concede the question—at least for the time being. But I'm still pondering another conundrum. Right now, I've kept the entire idea for a party from Damien, and that's a pretty big secret. But the second I tell him that we're going to head to Santa Barbara next Friday, he's going to assume it has to do with his birthday.

Even if he doesn't expect a party in our suite, he's still going to know that the trip is for him. And that means that even if I do take him out for a supposed birthday dinner, he's got his birthday on his mind, and some part of him— some tiny, minuscule part of him—isn't going to be as surprised by the party as I want him to be.

"So I don't know what to do," I add, after explaining all of that to my friends.

"He's going to love it no matter what," Syl says. "Because you're the one throwing the party."

"I know," I say. "And I know I'm being way too persnickety. I just really want it to be special." I get off my chaise and go to the rail, then look down at the lawn where Damien is pushing five-year-old Ronnie on the swings. I can hear her squeals of laughter mixed with, "Higher, Uncle Damie! Higher!" and can't help but smile.

Sylvia comes up to me carrying the baby, Jeffery, who's sucking on the ear of a bedraggled bear. "He looks good down there. When are you guys going to have one of your own?"

"Someday," I say, taking Jeffery from her in a not-so-subtle attempt to keep the conversation off the state of my uterus. "In the meantime, I'm just going to be the best aunt ever. Aren't I, little man?" I ask as I lift him up and make silly faces. "Aren't I the best aunt in the whole, wide world?"

Beside me, Syl laughs. At the same time, Cass says, "Why don't you just pull a double-blind?"

I turn to her, so grateful that she's firmly changed the subject I could kiss her.

"What's that?" I ask, as I go to sit in the shade with the baby.

"It's simple. You just set up a dummy event."

"Like taking him out for dinner," I say. "But he'll still know that it's a birthday dinner."

Cass shakes her head. "No, no. You have to back off from birthday shenanigans completely."

I glance over at Jamie, who's sitting next to me, but she just shrugs, obviously as clueless as I am.

"Okay, listen." Cass stands up, obviously getting into her spiel. "Your whole problem is that you don't want him to have a clue as to why you're going to Santa Barbara, right?"

"Right," I acknowledge.

"So *tell* him you're going. And have the reason be something completely unrelated to his birthday."

I nod slowly, letting the idea play out in my mind. "That's actually kind of brilliant."

"It really is," Jamie agrees.

"So I just have to get all the guests there, keep everyone quiet, don't let Damien have a clue, and then actually surprise him."

"Pretty much," Cass agrees.

"It's so deviously simple. I can't believe I didn't think of it myself."

"I'm all about the devious," Cass says, pretending to buff her nails.

"Double-blind." I let the words roll softly off my tongue as I look around the patio at my friends. Then I grin and raise my mimosa in a toast. "Ladies, I think we have a plan."

"Well, yeah," Siobhan says. "But you still need to come up with the reason."

Chapter Four

I'M STILL TRYING to craft a fake reason for a trip to Santa Barbara when Damien calls for Edward to drive all of us home. We're not drunk, but the mimosas and Bloody Marys definitely flowed, and it seems the prudent thing to do.

While we wait for him to arrive with the limo, Damien and I help put the kids down. First Jeffery, who listens with big eyes while Damien reads *Goodnight, Moon*, and then Ronnie, who insists on reading a Dr. Seuss book to me.

When she's quiet in bed with Bun-bun, I pad out into the hall to join Damien, Sylvia, and Jackson.

"You've got a knack," Sylvia says, with a hint of a tease in her voice.

"And a great deal," I point out. "As a card carrying member of the Favorite Aunt Society, I don't have to discipline, I get to spoil them rotten with toys, and I can fill them up on junk food with impunity. What's not to love?"

Sylvia laughs, and I glance at Damien. He's smiling, but there's also a wistful look on his face that makes my heart squeeze a little. He sees me watching him, and reaches for my hand.

I take it, lacing my fingers with his.

"Come on," he says. "Let's go home."

What I hear is, "I love you."

"Yeah," I say. "Let's go."

By the time we all get our things gathered, Edward's waiting in front of the house. He drops off Cass and Siobhan in Venice Beach first, then heads to Studio City to drop Jamie and Ryan.

"Be good," Jamie trills as they get out of the limo. "Of course, we don't intend to be." She waggles her brows and laughs as Edward shuts the door.

"You heard the lady," Damien says, pulling me close to him.

I lay down on the seat with my head in his lap. "You know me. I'm a big fan of alone time in limousines. But it's a short ride to the Tower—and right now, I'm very, very comfortable."

I open my eyes to study his face, looking down at me with a definite spark. I laugh. "A day in the sun with kids. I'm exhausted. Aren't you exhausted?"

His smile blooms slowly—and very sensually. "Just how exhausted are you?"

A warm current wafts through me. "I could be revived," I admit. "If I was made a good offer."

"So we're negotiating. Excellent. I'm sure I have something you want." His hand closes gently over my breast, and I arch up, gasping from the impact of a sudden, hard flash of desire.

"Damien."

His brow rises infinitesimally. "See? I'm confident we'll be able to come to a mutually satisfactory agreement."

His thumb grazes my lower lip, and I close my eyes, drawing it in, reveling in the sound of pleasure he makes low in his throat and the erection I feel growing where the back of my head is in his lap.

"I could just roll over," I say, doing exactly that, so that my ear is on his thigh and I'm facing the button on his jeans.

I lift my hand and press lightly over the length of his erection straining against the denim right in front of me. "Think how much faster the rest of the drive would be."

"Nikki." There's a tightness in his voice. Almost a warning. But I don't heed it. Frankly, I don't think he wants me to. Slowly, I stroke my hand up the length of him, a wild knot of heated need growing inside me, spreading wilder and faster as I feel him harden beneath my hand. As I hear the shift in his breathing. The catch in his throat when my hand reaches the base of his cock and then rises to the button of his jeans.

"Christ."

That's all he says, and I turn my head just enough so that I can see the desire in his eyes. A wild lust. A wanton need that matches my own. There's never a moment when I don't crave this man, but right now—after a day in the sun with the alcohol still warming my blood—I think that I will die if I can't touch him. Can't taste him.

And with every second that passes—with every tiny shift in his posture, every shortened breath, every tightening of his muscles as he fights for control—I know that I am winning. And that rush of power that courses through me is as potent as wine and as powerful as the most magical aphrodisiac.

It takes some doing, but I manage the button with one hand. The zipper is trickier, and I try to hurry because Damien has lifted his hand, and I'm afraid that if I don't manage, Damien will do it himself, and this is something that I want. Wholly and completely.

But it's not his fly that Damien is reaching

for, it's my leg. And as I lower his zipper, his hand slides slowly up my leg, slipping under the hem of my skirt so his palm rubs my bare skin.

I shiver as I ease his zipper down, then slide my hand in and stroke his cock though his briefs. He's so damn hard, and I slowly ease the fly open to free him. His erection springs free, and I move forward just enough so that I can run the tip of my tongue lightly over the head as his hand squeezes my thigh tighter and tighter.

"Nikki, fuck, baby, that feels amazing."

I allow myself a smug smile before I move forward even more and tease the tip of my tongue along the underside of his cock, all the way from balls to tip.

As I do, his free hand slides up the back of my neck and I feel the pressure of his thumb as I slowly draw in his cock, deeper and deeper until I feel it in he back of my throat. Until his hips start to shift under me in a subtle demand that I suck him hard, deeper.

His fingers slide further up my leg, then slip under my panties. "Spread your legs," he orders, his voice like heated sandpaper. I try, but it's not easy in my awkward, sideways position. It's enough, though, and soon his fingers are stroking me. I'm wet and slick, and I shift position, pressing against his hand, wanting more and more—and then gasping when he thrusts his fingers deep inside me, mimicking the way I'm taking his cock in my mouth.

He finger fucks me hard and deep, and I shamelessly ride his hand, my own mouth working the same rhythm on his cock as a wild, wanton pressure builds inside me.

I'm close—I'm so damn close. And my muscles tighten around him, drawing him in even as every cell in my body races closer and closer to release.

And then he withdraws, shocking me with the sudden cessation. I pull my head back, releasing his cock as I cry out in protest.

"On me," he orders as I struggle to catch my breath and swallow my protests. "I want to feel you shatter around me. I want to look in your eyes while you come. And I want to explode deep inside you."

I nod because words just aren't happening right now, and I start to pull off my panties while I rearrange myself so that I can move onto his lap.

"No."

I don't understand at first, but then his hand slides under my skirt again and he tugs the crotch aside as I straddle him. His cock is right there pressing against me, and I'm so turned on I don't want to wait. I lower myself, biting my lower lip as he fills me, then gasping as his finger inside my panties shifts just enough so he can tease my clit as I ride him.

"Hurry, baby," he murmurs. "We're almost there."

My head is fuzzy with lust, but I realize he means the Tower—not our orgasms.

With his other hand he cups my breast, and as I ride him faster and harder, his fingers tighten on my nipple, hard now under my thin bra and T-shirt. Tighter and tighter, and I moan and squirm and gasp as a delicious pressure builds inside me. And when I explode—when a wild, relentless orgasm rocks through me like a cresting, pounding wave—Damien releases my nipple and I feel a wild whipping heat crack through my body, tracing a line of indescribable intensity from my nipple to my clit, and deep, deep inside me.

"Damien," I beg. "Now. Please, now." Because we've arrived, and Edward is shutting off the engine, and any minute now he's going to open the limo door that's just a few feet from us. But no way am I getting off my husband until I've taken him all the way.

And just as that determined thought cuts through me, Damien clutches my hips, thrusts down even harder so that he fills me completely, leans his head back, and explodes.

For a moment, we stay like that, me straddling him and us both breathing hard. Then I hear Edward's footsteps and I scramble off, adjusting my skirt, and knowing full well that my panties are soaked through.

And by the time Edward opens the door, my clothes are back to normal and Damien's jeans are buttoned.

Damien grins at me, then ushers me out of the limo in front of him. I comply, though I don't look Edward in the eye. And it's not until we're in our private elevator that I finally relax, my nerves kicking in as I collapse against the side of the car, my body shaking with laughter.

"I swear I hadn't planned a repeat performance," I say as we step into the elevator.

"Complaining, Mrs. Stark?"

"On the contrary," I say as we begin to rise. "I was going to comment how very much I love limousines. They're very … invigorating. I'm hardly tired at all anymore."

"I'll keep that in mind."

"I was wiped," I admit. "Those kids exhausted me. I expected it from Ronnie. But I had no idea a baby could wear me out. Did you see how fast that kid can move?"

The elevator arrives, the doors opening on our foyer. I step out, and immediately kick off my shoes.

"He's got good genes," Damian says. "He'll be a little athlete, that one."

"I think Jackson's hoping for a little architect," I counter.

"I have every confidence in Jeffery. He can be both."

"Absolutely," I agree as I head toward the living room.

Damien takes my arm and tugs me back toward him. "Might be nice to have one around here." His voice is low. Almost tentative. And Damien is never tentative.

Something raw shifts in my chest, and I'm really not sure if it's a good or a bad feeling. "I thought you said you weren't drunk."

"I'm very sober." He holds my head with one hand and traces my lower lip with the index finger of the other. "They have good kids," he says softly. "We would, too."

"We would, yes." My voice is shaky. "But I just got invited to submit that proposal. My business is just getting off the ground."

"I know," he says.

"I don't want to put all that aside." My insides are tight, and my voice is rising in pitch. "And I haven't got a clue about how to be a mom. You know that."

"Hey," he says gently. "Calm down. I didn't say we should have kids tomorrow. Just some day. We've always said we'll have them some day."

I nod, a little relieved. A little embarrassed

that I overreacted. "Sorry. I just—"

"Of course, I am getting older," he interrupts with a definite tease in his voice.

I smirk. "Yeah, you're looking pretty decrepit these days. Is that your way of reminding me you have a birthday coming up?"

"Are you saying you need reminding?"

"Never." I sidle up closer, shaking off the lingering panic, then smile up at him. "So tell me, Birthday Boy. What would you like?"

"So many choices." He trails a fingertip down my arm. "Maybe a birthday strip tease?"

I raise my brow. "Interesting choice. I'll see if I can't hire someone."

"I'd rather have one from my wife."

"I'll keep that in mind."

"Maybe you should practice so it's perfect."

"Should I?"

He bends down so that his lips graze my ear. "Dance for me, baby. Right now."

"Is that what you want?" I ask. "To watch me dance? Because I have something else in mind."

His brow rises. "Do you?"

"Mmm," I say, then start humming as I pull out my phone and find my current favorite song on my workout playlist. A little fast. A little raunchy. A lot fun. I click the button to send it through our sound system, and when the music starts, I press my hand to Damien's chest and jauntily strut forward, forcing him backward to the padded bench that is intended as a place to sit and wait for the elevator. Right now, I have a different purpose in mind.

"I'll dance," I say, doing a shimmy and pulling off my T-shirt in the process. "I'll even do a stripper dance," I add. "But I don't do solo shows. I require full participation."

"Do you?"

"Absolutely," I say, turning around so that my back is to him as I shake and shimmy in time with the music and very, very slowly ease my skirt off.

When I turn around, I'm dressed only in my bra and panties, and though I should feel silly, I don't. Maybe it's the alcohol. Maybe it's the lingering high from fucking him in the limo. Maybe it's the heated way that he's watching my every move.

Maybe it's the simple fact that I love my husband.

Whatever the reason, I'm enjoying showing off, turning him on and getting turned on in the process. And as I think that, I slide one hand over my bra and the other down my abdomen to cup myself over my panties.

I have my eyes closed, and the music's loud, but I still hear Damien's sharp intake of breath. I figure that's as good a cue as any, and I open my eyes and strut toward him, then reach out a hand to pull him up.

He complies, amused, and I do my own version of a pole dance, with Damien playing the role of my pole. Up and down, stroking and teasing, shimmying and shaking. It's a little erotic and a little silly, and by the time I have my bra off and am about to step out of my panties, I'm both desperately wet and giggling furiously.

I bend over to untangle my panties from around my ankle, and when I do, my giggles turn to squeals as Damien scoops me up and tosses me over his shoulder. I pound uselessly on his back, then cry out when he pitches me unceremoniously onto the bed.

"What are you—?"

"Shhh." He puts his finger over his mouth, then strips off his own clothes. And though he doesn't add any dance moves, I can't deny that I enjoy the show.

Slowly, he eases onto the bed and straddles me. "I liked your dance," he says. "I like even more that you did it because I told you I wanted it."

"Anything you want," I whisper, my voice throaty. "You know that."

"I want you," he says, then brushes a kiss over my lips. "That's all I've ever wanted."

"You have me," I murmur. "You always have."

"I know." His smile is slow, his eyes dark with passion. "You're my proof that I must be a good man. How else could I deserve you?"

I blink, my eyes suddenly damp, and I pull him down for a long, slow kiss. "Make love to me," I beg. "And make it slow."

"Anything the lady wants," he says, sliding his hand down and finding me very, very wet. "I'm always happy to oblige."

We make love slowly, easily. And as he takes me over the precipice and my body shatters in his arms, I know without a doubt that I am loved as deeply and passionately as it is possible to be.

And, more, I love him back just as much.

Sated, I curl up against him, and I'm drifting toward sleep when Damien's voice rolls over me. "We should go to Vancouver for my birthday."

"Mmm," I say.

Then the words register on my sleepy brain, and suddenly I'm wide awake. I roll over, forcing myself not to curse. Surely—*surely*—he's not going to screw with all my planning. "Vancouver? Really? Why?"

"Because it's beautiful, and you've never been. And I want to show you the world."

It's an incredibly sweet thought, and if I weren't so frustrated that he voiced it, I might actually appreciate it. As it is, I just force a smile and say, "Then it should be my present. Not yours."

"That's one way of looking at it. But nothing makes me happier than spoiling you, Vancouver," he says firmly as he pulls me close. "I'll plan the perfect trip. I promise, you'll love it."

And as he drifts off, I stare at the ceiling, one single thought going through my mind.

Well, damn.

Chapter Five

AS THE ELEVATOR descends toward the Stark Tower lobby, I play back last night's conversation. *Vancouver.* How in the hell am I going to get out of going to Vancouver?

The car slows as it approaches the lobby, and I pull out my phone, watching the screen so that I can dial Jamie the second I get a signal. My best friend is devious, after all. Surely she can help me come up with a plan for forestalling Vancouver before Damien makes all the arrangements.

Either that or she'll talk me into forgetting the surprise altogether and going with the Damien-driven Canada plan.

"No way are you doing Vancouver," she says as I step off the elevator. I've whipped through my summary of last night's conversation, and she's as flustered as I am. "He only thinks he wants it because he doesn't know about the alternative."

"Agreed," I say. "But how do I get him to forget about his trip without telling him about the party?"

"I don't know. Tell him you have a deep-seated hatred of Vancouver. Tell him your mom made you do a beauty pageant there or something."

I grimace. That would work, actually. Damien would happily sacrifice a vacation if he thought that the destination was haunted by my bad memories.

"The problem is that I actually want to see Vancouver someday. It's supposed to be beautiful. And if I tell him that, I'll never get to go."

"Ah, well, in a year or so you could tell him that you want to bravely conquer your demons, and that you should both go up to Vancouver to face your bad memories."

I rub my temples. "Just think about it, okay? And let me know if you have any ideas."

"No problem," she says. "Seriously. I'm off this morning. I'll brainstorm ideas."

"Thanks," I say. Then I add, "*Real* ideas, James," before I hang up.

I pause in the lobby and look around. I'd been so frazzled this morning, that I'd left the apartment without my usual travel mug of coffee, which is why I'd stopped at the lobby instead of heading straight into the parking structure.

Unfortunately for me, the line at Java B's is at least a mile long, and I consider heading back upstairs and coaxing a latte from our espresso machine. But I honestly don't have the energy, and so I use the time to scroll through my emails, trying not to think about the Vancouver conundrum, and instead simply operating on the premise that if I just ignore, it will all go away.

"Nikki?" My name is pronounced with a thick, familiar accent.

I look up, unable to place the voice, and find myself looking at the stunningly beautiful face of Carmela D'Amato, an Italian super-model who also happens to be Damien's former girlfriend. She's just picked up her coffee, and she holds it in one hand while she pushes a strand of silky dark hair behind her ear with the other.

She takes a step toward me, smiling bright-ly, and I return her smile automatically even as I cringe and wish that I had an escape plan. But she looks so genuinely pleased to see me that I want to kick myself for being a bitch.

Yes, there'd been a period there when I'd thought Carmela was the devil. But things have changed, and we've come to an understanding of sorts. She's hardly my bestie, but I'm no longer afraid she's trying to screw my husband—or screw with me.

"It's great to see you," I say after she releases me from a hug so enthusiastic that I fear she's going to spill coffee down the back of my pale blue dress. "I'm sorry if I seem off—I'm just surprised. I thought you were in London these days."

"I am. I have the most darling townhouse just off Portabella Road. You and Damie must come to London so we can spend time. He has an office there, yes? And surely he hasn't sold the house in Maida Vale? But even if he has, you will stay at a hotel, or even with me. I will take you around to all the best designers. It will be a girls' weekend, yes?"

Her enthusiasm is infectious. "Sounds fun," I admit. "Maybe one day we can make it happen."

"I will tell Damie that you agree, and that the two of you must come as soon as it is possible."

"Tell Damien?" I suddenly realize what I'd apparently been blocking. "Of course, you're here to see him."

Her mouth shifts into a thin line, and for a moment I'm afraid that she thinks I'm jealous. But then I see that it's not anger or irritation in her face—it's fear and frustration.

"Carmela?" I reach out and touch her arm. "Hey, what is it?"

She blinks, and a tear clings to her long lashes before falling onto her cheek. "Forgive me. I am—I do not like having to pull you back into this. I do not like that it is my fault, too."

"What's your fault?"

"Those photos," she says, her voice so thick I can barely understand her. "Those wretched blackmail photos of Damie and me."

"OKAY," I SAY, pacing in front of the reflecting pool that is the centerpiece of the Stark Tower plaza. "Let me get this straight."

Since I'd foregone my coffee to take her outside and get to the bottom of this, I'm not thinking as clearly as I'd like. She'd run me through the whole convoluted story, but I want to make sure I really understand what's going on.

"You're telling me that your manager is the one behind that blackmail attempt?"

She nods from her perch on the edge of the pool, looking miserable.

I exhale and run my fingers through my hair. Not long after Damien and I were married, someone had tried to blackmail Damien by threatening to release some extremely racy photos of him and Carmela. What had made it worse was that the blackmailer had also gotten a hold of explicit pictures of Jamie with her next-door-neighbor.

Thankfully, Damien had put the fear of god into the anonymous blackmailer, and the pictures weren't released.

But then about a year ago, not long before Jeffery was born, the photos had turned up again—in the hotel room of my prodigal father, who'd just reintroduced himself to me.

At first, Damien had believed that Frank was behind the original blackmail attempt, but after Frank's adamant denials and some investigative work, we'd all come to realize that the photos were planted in his room.

But we never learned by who or why.

The damn photos are like a bad penny, and I really don't understand why or how Carmela's manager fits in.

"Are you sure?" I ask, sitting down beside her. "Why? Why on earth would your manager want to blackmail you? Or Jamie, for that matter?"

"Because he is a horrible, vindictive, ambitious man."

I wait for her to elaborate, but she just sits by the pool pouting prettily as businessmen walk by, openly staring.

"Can you be more specific?"

She sighs and her forehead crinkles. "He

has always been my manager, from when I was very young. It is much easier to model when you are young, no? And I am in my thirties now, and that is not so good for a model. Bertrand knows this, and so as I neared thirty, he tried to get me roles in the cinema."

"You did a few movies, didn't you? Italian films, and a few small Hollywood roles, too." Jamie had mentioned seeing Carmela on screen once or twice. At the time, I hadn't paid attention, because that was before our truce. Now, I'd probably watch one of her films.

"A few," she confirms. "But I was not a star in either country, and Bertrand thought this was a terrible travesty. I will tell you a secret—it is not a travesty. I am not an actress. I do not like it, and I am not pleasant to watch. It is not my dream, and yet it was his. So he pushed and pushed, and I have always trusted him, and so I let him guide me."

"Let him bully you," I say, and she lifts a shoulder in acknowledgement.

"But what does that have to do with the photos?"

"He was going to release them, thinking the scandal would help my career. He did not care that it would hurt you or Damien. He thinks only of himself."

I sit, shocked, as that bit of information washes over me.

"You knew about it?" I finally say. "All this time, you've known?"

She stands up, looking as shocked as if I'd slapped her across the face. "No! That is why I am here. I have only just learned all of this. Please, Nikki, you must believe me. I knew nothing."

"I do," I say. "I mean, I did. I thought you were confessing now, and—"

"No," she says, her voice hard. "I would never do such a thing."

"Okay. Sorry. I believe you."

She nods firmly, but doesn't continue.

"I can kind of understand the whole scandal thing and why he might think that would drive your career. But why Jamie?"

"Two reasons. He thought that photos of just me and Damie would be suspicious. And he was also expanding his business to America. He was looking for clients. And wouldn't a young actress caught in a scandal need his guidance?"

I frown—and realize my hands are clenched into fists so hard my fingernails are cutting into my palms.

"Is he the one who planted the photos on my father?"

She sits again, nodding miserably. "I am not sure what Bertrand was thinking about that. But your father is an excellent photographer. I understand he shoots mostly landscapes now, but he has done runway coverage, too, and he is very talented."

I believe that. I've seen my father's portfolio, and though travel photography is his passion, he has an excellent eye overall.

"He shot some portraits of a model who is on Bertrand's list. She wanted to leave him, and so was building her own portfolio."

"Bertrand never pushed that," I point out, because there was never a threat about the photos found in my father's room.

"The model—she was killed in a traffic accident. I do not know if Bertrand would have pushed against your father if she had not died."

"I'm sorry," I say. "Did you know her?"

Carmela nods. "She was very sweet and very young." She swipes at her eyes again. "Anyway, as I said, I knew none of this. At least not until last month."

She glances at her watch. "We should go up and tell this all to Damie, too. I am supposed to be there at ten. I spoke with—ah, Reagan? She said she would squeeze me in."

"Rachel," I correct. "Let me ask you this— is your manager threatening to release the photos today?"

She shakes her head, "No. No, he knows I found them, and he told me the whole story. He doesn't plan to release them." She licks her lips. "At least so long as I play nice. That is how he said it. *Play nice.*"

"Sounds like a charming guy. Hang on."

I pull my phone out. "Hey, Rach, it's Nikki. I'm sitting here with Carmela. Can you move her appointment with Damien to tomorrow? Same time?"

Rachel, fortunately, doesn't ask any questions. Carmela, of course, does.

"But I need to see him," she says. "I need his help. I do not want to play nice, and who better than Damien to play—what is the saying?—hard ball?"

"Totally with you. But humor me, okay? It's probably stupid, but I think I have an idea. And if I'm right, it'll help both of us."

"Help you?"

I stand and start pacing again. "Let me think this through. Bertrand told you everything? Why?"

She sniffles. "I went to his house. We have known each other for many years, and I thought he deserved a discussion between friends when I left him as a manager."

"So you were firing him?"

"I have no wish to model anymore, and I do not want to act. There is no business between us moving forward, though I had no ill thoughts toward him. I went to his house believing that he had always had my best interests at heart. That he was eager and aggressive, but that he wanted me to be a success. I thought he would be happy for me."

"So you were leaving for some other kind of job entirely?"

"New job. New life." Her smile lights up the morning and she holds out her left hand, revealing an engagement ring that I can't believe I hadn't noticed, because the stone is roughly the size of a small apple. "Paolo is a brilliant fashion designer. We will work together, and I will have my own couture line."

"Congratulations," I say. "On both counts."

"He is very charming. And," she adds with a wink, "he is at least as handsome as your Damie."

"I highly doubt that," I say, a smile twitching on my lips.

She laughs. "You are right, of course. But don't tell Paolo," she adds in a low whisper. "I am still one of the greatest models of this generation, no? I cannot marry a man prettier than I am."

Now I do laugh out loud. "Okay, okay, so we have to get back on topic." I'm thinking I may take her up on the trip to London. I'm liking Carmela more and more. "So he was pissed that you were firing him. And then, somehow, you found the photos?"

"He actually showed them to me. He told me everything. And then he said that if I didn't want Paolo and the world to see the pictures, I would continue to let him represent me in the couture business. And that Paolo and I would book all our models through him, and—"

I hold up a hand. "I get it. Obviously, you don't want Paolo to find out."

"No, that does not bother me. I told him. I even showed him—I took a photo of the print with my phone."

I nod slowly, processing all this. "You once told me that you'd cope if the photo got out. I think what you said exactly was that it would be embarrassing, but at least you looked damn good."

Her mouth quirks up. "It is true. The photo is explicit—but it is also very flattering."

"And Paolo doesn't mind?"

"He is thrilled to have a fiancée who is so delicious."

"Then you're here to protect Damien."

She nods. "And you," she says. "But also Paulo's family. He is fine with the photo being public. But his mother is very conservative. And his sister has taken Holy vows. They are welcoming me to the family, but I know that I am a bit of a scandal to them, you see?"

"I get it. And I have an idea. Is Paolo in LA with you?"

"Yes. Of course."

"And Bertrand. Could you get him to come to California by Friday? Specifically Santa Barbara?"

"I—well, yes. He is already in Los Angeles for meetings. So, yes. I think I can do that. Why?"

"Carmela," I say, "I want to invite you and Paolo to Damien's birthday party next Friday."

She blinks, obviously confused. "We—we would be delighted. But what does that have to do with—"

"Everything," I say, as I sit down beside her again. "I have this plan…"

Chapter Six

"I'LL FUCKING KILL him myself," Jamie says after I've relayed everything that Carmela told me that morning.

"I think I'd like a piece of that action. And I know Damien would. But I wasn't actually thinking homicide. You're in, though, right? You and Ryan? Because I need Ryan on my side at the meeting tomorrow."

"Not a problem. Ryan is going to be so stoked to take that fucker down."

We're window shopping in the Beverly Center, and I've been letting the whole Carmela problem gel. If my plan works, I'll get Damien to Santa Barbara instead of Vancouver, solve my double-blind problem, and also help Carmela by shutting Bertrand's blackmail scheme down cold.

Ambitious, yes. But the pieces are coming together.

Of course, I now realize that Jamie and

Ryan have to be in on it, too. Bertrand only threatened Carmela with the photos of her. But the bastard still has Jamie's pictures. And, frankly, I think he needs to meet with a little of Ryan's wrath.

"And now that we're all set on the extortion side of the equation," I say, "let's turn back to the equally important task of finding a birthday present for my husband."

"Sexy lingerie?"

I shoot her a sideways look. "I'm shopping for Damien, not me."

"Well, obviously. What girl wears sexy lingerie if it's not for the guy? Without a guy it's all snuggly flannel or soft cotton or totally ripped up sleep shorts and a threadbare T-shirt."

I have to concede that she has a point. "Still, I was thinking of something to give him. Not to wear for him."

"Well, I don't have a clue."

Neither do I, which is why we're at a mall instead of one of the smaller, locally-owned boutiques where I prefer to shop. I'm hoping that wandering aimlessly through a shopping nirvana will jump-start my creative, present-buying mojo.

So far, my mojo is less than enthusiastic.

"A tie? Cuff-links? A really excellent walking stick?"

I just raise my brows.

"I'm only trying to be helpful."

"Try harder," I say, then laugh when Jamie sticks her tongue out at me.

"He is absolutely the hardest person in the world to buy for," Jamie says.

"Tell me about it."

"Just go with the party and call it a day," she begs. "I want to get over to El Coyote and have a drink before dinner."

"I could get him a book," I muse. "A first edition Asimov or Bradbury? One he doesn't already have, of course." Damien loves sci-fi, and he has a small collection of first editions from his favorite authors.

"Not bad," Jamie concedes. "We could go grab a drink and then hit Mystery Pier, that really cool bookstore by Whiskey A Go Go."

"I think it's closed now," I point out.

"Then we just get the drink."

I bump her hip. "Would you stop? We'll be at dinner soon enough."

"Drinks after?"

Now she's just being a goof. "You're going to have to settle for margaritas when we meet Wyatt. I'm booked after."

"Really? I kinda thought we'd hang out to-night. I mean since Ryan's working late. And Damien's in Palm Springs. What's he doing, anyway?"

"He went out with Jackson. Something about that retail center they're building. They're meeting the contractor in the morning."

"See? You need company."

I laugh. "Sorry. I told Evelyn I'd stop by on the way home. And after that, I'm digging in on my proposal."

"For that company in Dallas?"

I nod, and she makes a face. "What?"

"Just you actually going out of your way to go back to Dallas. This might be one of the signs of the apocalypse."

I roll my eyes, but the truth is, she's right. Hell, I'd almost declined to submit a proposal for that very reason. But I'd pushed through, and told myself it was too good an opportunity to pass up. "It's a global company in the downtown area of a very big city. It's not like I'll be moving back there. And I sure as hell don't have to visit my old neighborhood."

"Hey, if you're cool, I think it's great. Seriously."

"Thanks," I say, though I can't deny that the conversation has watered my already planted seeds of doubt. "At any rate, you're welcome to come back to Malibu with me. We'll go to Evelyn's, and then afterwards, you hang out while I work. Lounge in the hot tub or the media room. We can have a couple of drinks after I finish if it's not too late, and you can crash in the guest suite."

She considers, but shakes her head. "Ryan's going to be late, but he's still coming home." She sighs loudly. "God, when did I get so domesticated?"

"It creeps up on you slowly," I say completely deadpan.

"Isn't that the truth? Anyway, tell Evelyn I said hi. And I still think the book idea is a good one. A really snazzy first edition would probably knock Damien's socks off."

"I'll pop in tomorrow if I don't come up with a more amazing idea in the meantime." I still want something with a little more oomph, but I'm also still completely lacking in ideas.

"An old-fashioned shave?" She points to The Art of Shaving, just a few doors down from where we're loitering. "Hot towels. A straight razor?"

Since that's not a terrible idea, I head that direction. We pass by a display of sexy lingerie, and I pause—because of course Jamie's put the idea in my head—and then I come to a complete stop, my hand reaching out to grip Jamie's wrist as ice courses through my veins.

"Jamie."

"Hey—shit, Nikki, what is it?"

"No," I whisper even as I whip around to face the reality I saw reflected in the window.

Mother?

But now that I'm turned around, there's nothing there. But I'd seen her. I'd *seen* her. Behind me. Near the escalator.

Didn't I?

"*Nikki.*" Jamie is yanking on my arm. "What the hell? Are you okay?"

I reach out blindly, my hand going to the glass front of the shop window. I lean against it and breathe in deep.

"Are you sick? Should I call Damien? *Shit*, he and Jackson are all the way in the desert."

"I'm okay." I hold up a hand. "It's fine. I just—I just thought I saw my mother."

"Your mom? She's in town?"

"It wasn't her. I must have just seen someone who looked like her. It freaked me out. Seriously, James. I'm fine." But I can't help but think that maybe I shouldn't submit the Dallas proposal after all.

Jamie screws up her mouth. "I believe you. I just think if you're going to freak out over a mirage, it should be something more interesting than your mother."

"Can't argue with that." I suck in a gulp of air, then push away from the wall and run my fingers through my shoulder-length hair. "Let's get out of here," I say firmly. "I'm starving."

EL COYOTE IS one of my favorite divey restaurants in LA, and is about the closest thing to Tex-Mex I've been able to find since moving from Dallas. That's not saying a lot—apparently there is a law that Tex-Mex can really only be found inside Texas—but the food is delicious and the atmosphere easy-going and fun.

As usual, the place is packed. I hand my keys to the valet, and Jamie and I walk through the parking lot toward the entrance together. I hesitate before we go inside. "You're not going to drive him screaming from the restaurant by asking him about his grandmother, are you?"

"Oh, please. Give me a little credit."

I just stare her down until she raises her hands in surrender. "No, I won't harass Wyatt."

"Good. Because I need him to do this favor, and if he bolts, I can't run after him in these shoes."

"Sure you could," she says, glancing at my feet. "I mean, honestly, Nicholas, if you can't run in wedges, you have no business living in Los Angeles."

I snort, then lead the way inside. I'm looking around to see if Wyatt has beat us there when he texts that he's about five minutes away and to order him a margarita.

"That's why I like him," Jamie says. "He

gets straight to the heart of the matter."

The hostess leads us to a booth with a view of the door, we order our drinks, and the bus boy brings chips and salsa. We both dive in, and for a moment we're both quiet. Then she looks up at me and says, "Not even one little question? I mean, he's the one who dropped the bombshell about his family. That's like opening a door."

"James," I say sternly. "Forget it."

The truth is, I'm curious, too. Wyatt had recently mentioned to Sylvia at a party that his grandmother is Anika Segel, a classically beautiful Hollywood legend from a powerful Hollywood family. In other words, Segel is an important name in this town, but Wyatt doesn't trade on that currency at all.

So, yeah. I want to hear the story, too.

Today, however, is not the day.

She exhales loudly. "Fine. Fine. I'll be good." The waitress brings our margaritas on the rocks, and she downs half of hers in one gulp. "I'm just looking to nail a juicy Hollywood story. Do you think Jane could get me on-set to interview Lyle Tarpin?"

Jane Sykes is a friend who recently had her book adapted into a movie, and Lyle Tarpin is a former sitcom star turned A-lister who's starring in it. "One, I don't think there is a set anymore. I'm pretty sure they're either editing or completely done. The premiere's just a few months away. And two, what is up with you? You just landed the weekend anchor job. I thought you loved it. What's with the scramble to get Hollywood interviews?"

"I do love it," she says. "But it's all behind a desk. And it's local news. Which is fine, but—"

"You want to do the entertainment stuff," I finish for her. "I get it. Why not just ask Tarpin directly," I say with a shrug. "He's coming to Damien's party. Dallas and Jane are, too."

"Really? You'd be cool with that? And I can ask Wyatt then, too?"

"Wyatt too, what?" The man himself says as he slips into the booth beside me. "Hello, ladies."

"Thanks for coming," I say, and since I'm now thinking of his Hollywood heritage, I can't help but notice that he has the looks that go with the pedigree. A classic, angular face. Wind-swept golden-brown hair. And the kind of build that fills out a suit quite nicely.

Seriously, the guy could totally have followed in the family footsteps.

"It's been too long," I add. Wyatt gives Sylvia and me photography lessons on occasion. He's an excellent teacher, but we've all been so busy lately that we haven't done a session in months.

"It really has," he says, reaching for his margarita. "So? Wyatt, too, what?" he says again.

"I'm looking to pump up my cred at work," Jamie says. "I thought an interview with Anika Segel's grandson would be just the ticket."

"Jamie!"

"What? He asked. Twice."

I glower at her and take a gulp of my drink.

Wyatt laughs. "You know I adore you, Jamie, but no. That's not a connection I exploit."

"Oh." She frowns, obviously flummoxed, and I shove a chip into my mouth to hide my amusement. Jamie is rarely flummoxed.

"But ask me again in a couple of months. I won't talk about my family, but I may have something else going that you'll be interested in."

"Oh! Cool! What?"

But he just laughs.

"You're a saint," I tell him. "I would have just kicked her in the shins."

"He *asked*," she repeats, then turns to Wyatt. "She's afraid if I bug you then you won't do a favor for her. But what she forgets," she says, now looking at me, "is that Nikki's the kind of girl everyone wants to do favors for."

Wyatt laughs, and I considering sliding under the table and biting Jamie's ankles. "She has you there," he says to me. "What's the favor?"

I take a second, hoping my cheeks will stop burning, then dive in. "First off, I want to invite you to Damien's surprise party. Second, I don't suppose you've ever done fashion photography?"

"A bit," he says. "I worked for a couple of years in Milan. But that was a lifetime ago. Why?"

"I was hoping you'd want to do it again? Just for old times' sake. Actually, that's not quite right. I was hoping you'd pretend to do it. It's all part of a scheme to stop a blackmailing rat bastard. And I was kind of hoping you had a contact at one of the magazines."

For a moment, he looks confused. Then a devious smile plays at the corners of his mouth revealing a set of trademark Segel dimples. "Why the hell not?" he says. "I'm always up for an adventure."

Chapter Seven

"YOU'RE A CARD-CARRYING saint," Evelyn says. "You know that, right?"

I'm still feeling the margaritas as I sit with Evelyn Dodge on her back balcony watching the moonlight sparkle on the waves crashing on the beach below. It's the view that introduced me to Los Angeles. And re-introduced me to Damien, and I can't help but smile as I remember how that party ended up playing out. Me in the backseat of a limo, and Damien's voice wreaking havoc with my senses. Not to mention my body.

Evelyn chuckles. "I know that expression. You're thinking of your husband, and my words are just floating away into outer space."

I flash an apologetic smile. "Sorry. I was just remembering that party you threw to show off Blaine's artwork."

"Ah, yes," she says. "The party that started it all. Well, I can't fault you for thinking of that night. But I damn sure can't understand why you want to help that bitch with a stick up her ass."

"Carmela? She grows on you," I say.

Evelyn snorts. "Like mold." That's why I love Evelyn. She hasn't the faintest idea how to mince words.

She shifts in her chair, her lips pursed together as if she's searching for something. "I suppose she's tolerable, now that I don't have to see her every goddamn day. That little bitch was quite the prima donna back in the day." Evelyn was Damien's sports agent back when he was dating Carmela, so I can only imagine the stories she could tell.

"Oh, I'm sure she still is," I say, and Evelyn barks a laugh. "But she and I have come to an understanding. She keeps her hands off Damien and I keep my heel out of her ass." I flash a smile. "It works for us."

Evelyn snorts. "Now you're talking."

"Seriously, though, her manager's a raging prick. And I want to make sure those pictures of Damien and Jamie don't ever get released and Bertrand has the fear of god pounded into him. Or at least the fear of Damien and legal and financial demise. Will you help?"

She turns around, looking at a serving cart that sits on the patio behind us. "Of course I'm in." She sighs. "Damn the boy, he didn't leave one goddamn ashtray."

She pulls out a cigarette and lets it hang un-lit between her lips. "Blaine's determined that I give up smoking."

"I thought you'd already given it up."

"Well, yes. But not in my own house when he's not even in the damn country. What exactly do you need me to do?"

It takes me a second to realize she's talking about the Carmela problem and not about smoking. "Honestly, I just need you to come up to Santa Barbara on Friday. With Charles, too, actually," I add, referring to Damien's attorney, who's also one of Evelyn's good friends.

Evelyn leans back in her seat. "All right, Texas. Spill. What exactly are you up to? And what the hell do you need me and Charles for?"

"Actually, where Carmela's concerned, you're kind of a diversion. I want you in Santa Barbara for Damien's surprise party. I just don't want him to know why you're really there." I smile, feeling pleased with myself. "So I'm giving you guys a part to play in the Bertrand smackdown. But it's all part of a double-blind."

"I always knew you were clever, Texas. And this will keep those pictures of Damien out of the tabloids?"

"That's the plan."

"Then you know you can count both me and Charlie in."

I nod. I know how much she and Charles Maynard did to protect Damien's reputation back when he was still on the tennis circuit. A hell of a lot more than his father ever did, that's for sure.

"And Blaine's invited to the party, too, of course," I add.

She grinds her unlit cigarette into the tabletop as if she were stubbing it out. "Well, you can give his slice of birthday cake to someone else. The boy's in Asia for the rest of the month."

"Seriously?"

"He's the featured artist at one of Beijing's premier galleries. After the opening he's going to Shanghai and then Hong Kong and Tokyo."

"That's really great for him," I say.

"He's kicking ass and taking names, that boy." She smiles when she says it, but some of the pride I've heard before is lacking in her voice. "From what I see, your career's taking off, too."

"I'm trying," I admit. "I'm finishing a proposal right now for a Texas-based corporation with a global presence. It's the biggest job I've gone after." I think about the ghost of my mother I saw at the Beverly Center, and feel a quick stab of apprehension—and of anger. Because what should be an exciting opportunity is now tainted with dread simply because of my memories of that woman.

"I'm proud of you, Texas," Evelyn says, then reaches out and squeezes my hand. "I don't know what your competition is like, but I do know they'd be a fool not to take you seriously. I'm proud of you, and if that sounds patronizing, that's just too damn bad."

I laugh, my chest tight with emotions. "It doesn't sound patronizing at all." My own mother would probably tell me not to even bother, because I don't have a shot in hell.

I suck in a hard breath, trying to ward off weepiness. "I'm going to put the final touches on it, and then get Damien to read it tomorrow. He's so busy, I almost hate asking him, but—"

"Nonsense," she says. "For one thing, that boy would do anything for you. For another, it's nice to be needed." She sighs. "I used to be right in the thick of helping Blaine get ready for a show. But he's so tightly scheduled now and traveling so much, I just never—"

She cuts herself off with a shrug and a wave. "Doesn't matter. He's doing just fine without me."

"I—" I stop, afraid I'm crossing a line. But then I start over because I adore Evelyn, and where my friends are concerned, I don't back off. "Are you and Blaine okay?"

"Oh, hell, Texas, we're fine. He's taking off. It's what I've wanted for him for years. Honestly. I couldn't be happier."

"I'm glad," I say. But I'm not entirely sure I believe her.

"I SWEAR TO god, I will kill that fucker," Ryan says, as he paces in front of the huge window in Damien's office.

"If that is the plan," Carmela trills, "I do not object."

I've just finished summing up everything Carmela told me to Damien and Ryan.

Damien's on a couch in the sitting area, and kicks his feet up on the coffee table, his attention solely on me. "Carmela told you all of this yesterday?"

"We had a chat," I admit.

"And you're just now telling us this?"

"There wasn't an immediate threat that the pictures would get out," I say, looking to Carmela who nods in support. "And we wanted to have a plan."

"You didn't think to come to Ryan and me first? It's my ass out there—literally—and Ryan does have that handy Security Chief title. Not to mention a vested interest since his girlfriend's ass is equally exposed."

"Carmela and I already had an idea, and you were in Palm Springs with Jackson yesterday afternoon, and…" I trail off with a shrug, knowing I sound lame. The truth is that I would have brought Damien in on developing a plan if I wasn't trying to juggle two plans at once. One of which has to stay secret from him.

He rubs his temples. "Nikki—" He cuts himself off, looking perplexed. Not surprisingly; he knows me well enough to know this isn't the kind of thing I'd keep from him. Not without a good reason.

I really don't want him to figure out what my good reason is.

"Do not be cross with your wife, Damie. I begged her to help me come up with an idea to get the pictures from Bertrand and to make sure that he does not bother me—or any of us—again."

Damien exhales, then turns to Ryan, who shrugs casually. "Hey, fine by me. If they already have a plan in mind for shutting this guy down, let's hear it."

I smile gratefully at him, and he gives me the slightest nod in return. Jamie's told him the situation, of course, so he's playing along. And doing a damn good job, frankly.

"All right, then," says Damien. "Lay it out for me."

I stand and start organizing my thoughts.

"The idea is to get him to Santa Barbara thinking that Carmela's got a shoot for her couture line and that he's about to have a huge pay day. We have a photographer, an agent, and a magazine all set up already."

Damien's brows lift. "Do you?"

"Evelyn's pretty excited about cutting the balls off this asshole."

"I'll bet she is," he says, but his lips twitch, and I'm grateful he's amused and not pissed.

"We have an attorney, too. He's going to come with contracts that Bertrand supposedly has to review. Everyone goes through his suite, making arrangements and kissing his ass. And everyone we use is someone with serious clout in the industry."

"Let me guess," Damien says. "Evelyn's pulling Charles in. And Wyatt's in on the game, too."

"That's why you make the big bucks. You're so damn smart."

He lifts a finger and points it at me, and I know damn well what it means—*just wait until we're alone.*

I glance down at the floor to hide my grin. "Anyway," I conclude, "once Bertrand realizes it's all gone south, he'll also know that some heavy-duty names know who he is and what he's done. That's when you and Ryan do your thing. Lay out the ground rules and tell him that he either turns over the photos and leaves Carmela alone or the weight of all these people in your orbit will bear down on him."

"No police?" Ryan asks, presumably so that Damien knows we've thought this through.

"Too risky," I say. "The photos might get released to the press during the investigation."

"Agreed." He takes a seat opposite Damien. "I gotta say, I'm impressed. Maybe I should offer Nikki and Carmela a spot on my security team."

"Mmm," Damien says, in a way that makes me think that he may have already seen through all my maneuvering. I hope not. I want this party to be special. I want it to be a true surprise.

After a moment, he stands and goes to the window where Ryan had been only moments before. He looks out, then nods. "All right," he says, turning back to face the room. "We'll go with your plan. Evelyn is going to make the call to him, I assume?"

I nod. "She'll get him to Santa Barbara Friday morning, ostensibly for a sunset shoot. Friday's the earliest everyone can come together, and if we wait, we may run into more scheduling fiascos." I clear my throat. "I'm sorry about Vancouver. We'll have to cancel."

He looks at Ryan and then at Carmela. "Not a problem. Anything for my friends. I'm pretty sure Vancouver's not going anywhere."

"Damie, my pet, you are a prince." Carmela rises and glides across the room to him, then presses soft kisses to both corners of his mouth.

She pauses in front of me. "Nikki, darling, it is not personal," she purrs as I fight a laugh. "I am Italian, you know."

She heads toward the door with Ryan, and Damien and I follow. He closes the door behind them, then turns to me, his mouth opening to speak, but he doesn't get the chance. I'm right there, my mouth hard against his. His lips part, possibly in surprise, and I take full advantage, tasting and teasing and feeling the depth of the kiss right down to my toes.

"Well, hello to you, too," he says when I finally pull away, breathing hard. "I hope that was a reflection of your deep and constant lust for me, and not an indication that you have any lingering jealousy whatsoever about Carmela."

"Not jealous," I say, rising up on my tiptoes to press a gentle kiss to his lips. "I'm just glad that we're helping them. And," I add with a tiny little smile, "I want to make sure that when you walk out that door, it's me who's on your mind."

"Sweetheart, you're always on my mind."

Chapter Eight

I WATCH—A LITTLE nervous, a little excited—as Damien flips through the pages of my proposal, a red pen in his hand. It's eighty-three pages with the appendix, and Damien is going through it as slowly as a college professor reviewing a student's dissertation proposal.

I'm grateful for the attention to detail, but I'm also nervous as hell. Because I've poured my heart, my talent, and my experience into those pages, and what if Damien tells me it sucks?

Granted, he'll say it more politely, but in the end, crap is crap.

And—for better or for worse—Damien loves and respect me enough to tell me the truth.

Which explains why I'm fidgeting.

Which explains why Damien shoots me a look that very clearly says I should calm down.

And which also explains why I end up in

the kitchen pouring myself a glass of wine even though it's barely past lunch.

I putter around the kitchen, contemplating my frozen Milky Way stash and trying to think about anything other than his red pen, for at least half an hour, during which time my wine magically disappears.

The apartment is an open plan, but the kitchen is at an angle such that I can't see the sofa that Damien is sitting on, so I have no idea how much he's marked up those pages or if he's anywhere close to the end.

I'm seriously considering pouring another glass, when Damien steps into view and I suddenly feel like a schoolgirl about to be evaluated by the teacher.

He says nothing, and there's not even a hint of expression on his face. I can read this man so well, and yet in this moment I have no clue whatsoever what he is thinking.

The breakfast bar is between us, and I stand by the sink, my hands on the counter, and my first thought is that if he comes around to me, then it's bad news. Because that would mean he's coming to comfort me.

He pauses in front of the bar, and I exhale with relief. But then he keeps moving, circling into the main area of the kitchen, and I want to curl up and cry because I'd worked so hard on those damn pages, and how could I have messed it up that badly?

"Nikki," he says softly as he places his hands on my shoulders. Then he bends his head and kisses my forehead. "It's damn near perfect."

He must be able to tell that my legs have gone weak, because he closes his arms around me and pulls me close. I cling to him, my cheek pressed against his chest and my eyes closed in relief.

After a moment, I pull back, then peer at his face, trying unsuccessfully to read his thoughts.

"You mean it?"

His smile is slow, but I can see pride on his face, and it shoots right through me, the rush almost as exquisite as sex. "Oh, yeah," he says. "I mean it."

"So you think I have a shot."

He releases me, then crosses the kitchen and refills my wine glass before pouring one for himself. "More than a shot," he says as he hands my glass to me, then raises his in a toast. "To my brilliant wife and her burgeoning career."

"I'll drink to that," I say, then clink my glass against his. I take a sip, thinking about his support today and Evelyn's last night. "It's nice," I say softly, "knowing I have a safety net. People who'll watch my back and pick me up if

I crash. You. Jamie. Evelyn." I feel a tear trickling down my cheek and brush it away. "Anyway…"

"Nikki?" He tilts my chin up with his fingertip. "Baby?"

"I'm so glad you think it's good." I draw a shaky breath and force the rest of the tears back. "That means so much to me. But maybe I shouldn't submit it at all."

He cocks his head, studying me. "Because of Dallas?"

I lick my lips and nod. "I thought I saw my mother yesterday."

He stiffens. "What? Where?"

"It's okay," I say quickly. "I mean, it wasn't really her. I just—I don't know."

I'm completely exasperated with myself, and I step back so I can lean against the counter in front of the sink and look up at him. "I don't like feeling this way," I say, still clinging to Damien as I murmur the words against his chest. I feel edgy. Out of control and off center. And what I hate even more is that it's that woman who's making me feel this way. That even when she's not nearby, she's in my thoughts, like some horrible parasite that's made a home inside me.

I don't even realize that tears are streaming from my eyes until Damien takes one long stride, then enfolds me in his arms.

"Shhh," he says. "It's okay."

I gulp in air. "It is most definitely *not* okay." My mother is not someone I want to see in person, much less in my fantasies. I've spent too long fighting to get out from under her thumb. To forget the meals she wouldn't let me eat so that I wouldn't get "chubby." To overcome my fear of the dark, a fear that developed after nights locked in a pitch-black room because I had to have my beauty sleep. To literally battle my way out of the life she'd intended for me so that I could study engineering and computer programming. And, of course, to turn a deaf ear to her taunts that Damien couldn't want a useless girl like me, and that soon enough he would leave me for someone better.

"What if I get the job?" I ask, my voice thick with tears. "What if I see her in Dallas?"

"Nikki," he says, and I can tell from the tone of his voice that he hears so much more than my simple question. The insecurity. The fear. And the pulsing need to fight my way back to center any way I can.

A knife block on the kitchen counter catches my eye, and for one brief, shining moment, I imagine the blade on my skin. The pressure and then the pain. And then the release that feels like freedom.

It's only a split second before I wince and

turn away, but it doesn't matter; I know that Damien has followed both my gaze and my thoughts.

"Look at me" he says. I do, lifting my head to see the understanding in his eyes. "Is that what you need?"

"Yes," I whisper, because I can't deny the sharp longing that cuts through me. "Not a blade," I clarify. "But, yes. Please Damien. I need you."

It has been years since I've cut, but it doesn't matter. The need for the pain—for the release—is still in me; it always will be. I fight it daily—but I fight it best with Damien at my side.

Damien has always understood that need in me to find control in the pain. To use it to center myself. To calm the storm that would otherwise blow wild inside me.

I need to surrender. To let him walk me down that line between pleasure and pain, and take us both into ecstasy.

For a moment, he just looks at me. Then he makes a circular motion with his finger. "Turn around," he says. "Hands on the counter, and bend forward."

My pulse kicks up, and I hurry to comply. He's wearing fleece athletic pants tied loosely around his waist and nothing else, and as he steps behind me, I feel the material brush against my bare legs beneath my silk sleep shorts.

I also feel his erection pressing against my ass, and my body tightens with both desire and anticipation. Slowly, his hands trail up my thighs, then equally slowly, he hooks his thumbs in the waistband of my shorts and eases them down. I start to step out of them, but he swats my ass with one quick motion. "No," he says. "You don't move unless I tell you to."

I resist the urge to nod, but my lips curve into a smile. Since my back is to him, I figure that's okay. Right now, he can't see my face.

His fingertips dance along the curve of my rear, a slow torment that is not quite a caress and not quite a tickle. "Is this what you need?" he muses as his palm stings my rear. I bite my lip, not in pain, but so that I won't cry out that yes, yes, that is exactly what I need. That sharp impact, those brilliant red sparks. The sting that spreads out, filling me up before fading into a warm, soothing glow.

"Or maybe this," Damien suggests, running his fingertip down my crack and teasing my ass with his thumb while his fingers tease my core, but never enter me. "Should I take you like this? Hard and fast and with no warning?"

I whimper, and it takes all my effort not to gyrate my hips in a silent plea, because he's right *there*, and I want to feel him inside me. In that moment, it feels as though I might shrivel up and die if he doesn't just get down to it and fuck me right now.

"Or maybe both," he says, his words adding a new thrill even as I mourn the removal of his hand from between my legs.

"Spread your legs," he orders, backing away from me. I comply, and the cool air on my wet sex is so delicious that I moan a bit. He's no longer right behind me, and it's all I can do to resist the urge to turn around. I hear a drawer open and close, and then I feel something cool and flat against my bare skin. A spatula, I think. Or maybe a serving spoon.

"I'm going to turn your ass red," he whispers, and just the words alone make my cunt throb with wicked anticipation. He's bent over my back so that his lips are by my ear. He's taken off the sweat pants, and his erection is nestled between my legs, the slight friction as he moves freeing a wanton desire to curl through me.

His palm rubs my ass, and then the flat thing smacks against me, and I cry out in surprise more than pain. He soothes my rear with his palm, and I bite my lip, waiting for a second blow. And when this one comes, the sting is real and biting and so damn wonderful I feel as though it is swallowing me, wrapping me up in shooting stars, with Damien right there to grab me and lead me home.

"Baby," he murmurs as he slips his hand between my legs, his fingers slipping inside as he lands another blow. I cry out, my body clenching tight around his hand. "Nikki, god, Nikki. The way you respond to me. Do you know? Do you really understand? Everything I have. Everything I am, pales in comparison to the way I feel about you.

"I love you, baby," he continues as he tosses the spatula aside to clatter on the ground beside me, as he spreads my legs and thrusts hard inside me. "Anything you need. Anything you want. You will always have it. Forever, baby. I'm yours forever, and then some."

I feel my cheeks warm with tears even as my body spirals up and up. He's silent now, his body slamming over and over into mine. Possessing me. Claiming me. And, finally, destroying me in the sweetest way possible.

I break apart in his arms at the same time that he climaxes, and he clings to me, holding me tight, putting me back together, and leading me back to reality in his arms.

We slide to the floor together, and he holds me gently, then brushes a kiss over my temple.

"I'm sorry," I whisper, as I curl up next to him on the cold tile floor. "But thank you."

"Oh, baby, you know better than that.

Don't ever be sorry for what you need."

"I don't like feeling afraid. Feeling weak."

"It's not a weakness to need someone. If it were, I would be the weakest man on this earth, because I need you more than I can ever say."

I look up at him through tear-filled eyes, and the gentleness of his smile smooths away the last of my rough edges. I nod slowly, in understanding and agreement.

"And as for being afraid, there's nothing wrong with that. What matters is how you handle it."

I quirk my mouth. "Right now, the running away option seems reasonable. Forget the proposal. Never see Dallas again."

"But…?"

"But I want that job," I admit. "I at least want a shot at it. Damien, I can do the work, and I think my proposal will catch their attention."

"I know it will."

"But Dallas. My mother." I shiver. "I'll be walking through the ghosts of my old life. How can I do that?"

"You can do it because you're not alone. I'm right there with you, baby. And if there are ghosts, we'll fight them together. And I promise you, we'll win."

"I love you," I say.

"Oh, baby, I know. But I never get tired of hearing it."

Chapter Nine

T HE APTLY NAMED Pearl Hotel stands out like a gem even in a city as charming as Santa Barbara. The mission-style building gleams in the California sun, with two sparkling pools, burnished red roof tiles, and multiple rooftop patios with views of both the city and the white sand beach.

One of those patios graces the roof above the Presidential Suite, and as I stand at the railing, Damien's arms encircle my waist. I lean back against him and sigh deeply as I look out over the rooftops of nearby houses, a small park, and the ocean in the distance.

"I love it here," I say. "It's like an oasis in the middle of the city."

"At night it's even better," he says, as he looks out at the sun that still hangs well above the horizon. "Why don't we move the meeting with Bertrand earlier, then come back here in time to watch the sunset and have dinner here on the roof?"

"Tempting," I say, leaning back in the circle of his arms. "But too many moving parts. Ryan and Carmela and Wyatt, not to mention Evelyn and Charles for one. We're meeting them in just a few, remember? And Carmela if she can think of an excuse to sneak away from Bertrand."

It's just about time to dive into the Bertrand plan, and we're meeting to go over the plan one final time. And, of course, I have to consider all the puzzle pieces that Damien doesn't know about. Like the three dozen guests who are currently stashed away in their own rooms at this hotel or its sister property three blocks over.

They're staying out of sight until Damien and I are safely in Evelyn's room, which we're using as a staging area. As soon as we enter, Evelyn is going to call room service for cocktails. True, we want the drinks, but that will also be the cue for the concierge to not only call all the guests so that they can hurry to the Presidential Suite, but also to signal the event team to move in and set up the room.

In theory, it's going to go off like clockwork, and by the time everyone has played their part and Damien has laid down the law with Bertrand, the guests will be in place, the food will be set out, the decorations will be up, and Damien and I will walk through that door to a full-on, one-hundred percent surprise.

Just a few more hours, and I can stop worrying, because one way or another, the party will have started.

"All right," Damien says. His hands are around my waist, but as he bends his head so that he can press his lips to my ear, his hands slide higher to cup my breasts. "We'll just have to work with the schedule we have," he murmurs, his breath hot against my ear.

"Yes," I say, arching back as he cups my breasts and his tongue traces the curve of my ear. "We'll make do."

"Fortunately, I don't anticipate a long meeting. What I'm most looking forward to," he says, "is when we come back. I have very definite plans for the evening."

"Oh?" I say innocently.

"Oh, yes. First, I'm going to bring you back up here to the roof. Then I'm going to very slowly remove every bit of clothing until you're naked under the stars, the cool wind soothing on your hot skin. Then I'm going to have you stretch out on one of the chaise lounges, your eyes up toward the sky. Not that you'll see the stars, because I'll have a blindfold on you."

"Damien…" I'm not sure if I want him to stop or continue. All I know is that I'm already wildly aroused, and that we have to leave very,

very soon.

"Shhh," he says, pressing a finger over my lips. "Next, I'm going to tie your arms down. Then I'll spread your legs wide, your feet on either side of the chaise, so that you're wide open, baby. Open and hot and wet for me."

I swallow and squeeze my thighs together to quell a building need.

"Then I'm going to touch every inch of you without actually touching you. A feather. My breath. An ice cube…" He trails his finger down the side of my neck, and I have to reach out and hold onto the railing because my legs seem incapable of holding me up.

I whimper softly. Damien notices and smiles, the bastard.

"I'll run my fingertip over your skin next, paying special attention to your nipples. And then I'll kiss my way up your thighs, getting close, but never quite where you want me. Do you know why?"

"Because you're a cruel man?"

"Pretty much. Mostly because I want you desperate. I want you to beg me. And," he adds in a lighter tone, "because it's my birthday."

"Is it?" I ask innocently. "In that case, sir, I'm at your disposal."

He chuckles. "I like the sound of that. But right now, I think you have a scam to pull off. But," he adds, pulling me close enough that I can feel his erection pressing against me, "we'll be back here soon enough."

We will, I think. *But I won't be getting my rooftop seduction.*

I sigh.

I really, *really* hope that Damien enjoys the hell out of his party.

"HOW DID IT GO?" I ask, as Evelyn and Charles shut the door behind them. We're in Evelyn's suite, using it as our base of operations, and Damien, Ryan, Jamie and I have been waiting for the last twenty minutes for her and Charles to return.

"Brilliant," Evelyn says, pouring herself a glass of bourbon before sinking into one of the overstuffed armchairs. "He's familiar with both me and Charlie, so he was primed to believe I'm representing Wyatt and some of the lesser models for the catalog shoot. Wyatt's still in there, by the way. Bertrand wants some candids of him and Carmela behind the scenes."

I'm sitting on one of the stools by the kitchen island with Jamie beside me. Ryan and Damien are by the window, and though I may be projecting, to me they both already look forbidding.

Beside me, Jamie turns on the stool, looking between Charles and Evelyn. "He knew who both of you were, but he didn't think about Damien?"

It's a valid question. Evelyn was a very public representative for Damien back in his youth, and now it's no secret that they remain good friends. And Charles has been his primary attorney for at least as long. Considering Damien features so prominently in Bertrand's blackmail pictures, it's surprising he didn't make the connection.

But Charles just shakes his head. "Maybe he's a damn good actor, but I don't think so. I think having Wyatt's editor friend call first made the whole thing seem more legitimate. He wasn't thinking in terms of scamming or getting scammed. He was thinking about his bank account."

I nod, grateful that Wyatt had been able to coax a friend at one of the top fashion magazines into helping us. She'd called to tell Bertrand that she wanted to do a spread with Carmela during Fashion Week.

"And Carmela?" Damien asks. "She's still in with him?"

Evelyn nods. "She's playing the role brilliantly. Thrilled about her modeling comeback, but cold and standoffish to Bertrand." She shifts her attention to me. "Did she tell you she couldn't act? I'd say she's doing a fine job."

"In my experience, Carmela has a knack for acting in whatever manner will get her what she wants," Damien says with affectionate humor. "I think that trait is serving her well now."

"When are we going in?" Jamie asks.

"You're not," Ryan says. "It's just me and Damien."

"And Nikki," Damien adds. "She should be there for Carmela."

I meet his eye, and see just the hint of a smirk. Apparently he sees the irony in me being there for Carmela as much as I do.

Jamie takes a step toward Ryan, undoubtedly to argue the point, but I grab her arm. "If you're there, he's going to be even more defensive," I say. "Besides, you can stay here with Evelyn and Charles. Hang out. Go get a drink. We'll find you when we're done," I say, looking her straight in the eye so that there's no way she can miss that what I mean is that we'll find her in my suite. Because that's where she's supposed to go next, to organize the party for Damien.

She crosses her arms and makes a face, but she nods. Then she pokes me in the chest. "You owe me one."

"Definitely," I say.

She flops back down on the couch. "So

when are y'all going in?"

"Carmela's supposed to call here, pretending to call room service." I glance at my watch. "Should be soon," I say, and the words are barely out of my mouth when the phone rings and Carmela places her fake order for a pitcher of martinis.

"Show time," Ryan says, and Damien takes my hand.

Bertrand's suite is one floor up, and we take the stairs. Carmela opens the door, her eyes wide, and leads us back into the parlor where Wyatt stands by the window, and Bertrand—a pudgy-faced man with a sour expression—sits at the desk, though he stands the moment he sees us.

"What the hell?" He whips around to find Carmela, who's moved near Wyatt. "What the fucking hell are you doing bringing that asshat and his little bitch here?" he rants, gesturing toward me and Damien. "And who the fuck is the flunky?"

Ryan steps forward. "The flunky can kick your ass without breaking a sweat," he says. "And the flunky is here to make sure none of these pictures—or any other similar pictures you might have squirreled away—get released."

He tosses a folder onto the desk, the impact causing the photos inside to slide partially out. They're the original blackmail photos we'd received back when this nightmare started. "Those see the light of day," Ryan says, "and you'll learn the meaning of regret the hard way."

To her credit, Carmela stands up straighter. "You see? They're here to help me, Bertrand. You wouldn't listen to me. Maybe you'll listen to them."

"What? You think I don't listen? How do I not listen? You tell me you want a career? Haven't I gotten you a career? I made you—and this is how you repay me?" He points suddenly to Wyatt. "You—Jimmy Olsen—get your ass out of here. You think I want this little confab recorded on film?"

Wyatt glances at Damien, who nods, then quietly leaves the room.

"The lady's interested in terminating her relationship with you," Damien says as soon as Wyatt's out of the room. His voice is calm, but I can see the tension.

"That true, baby?" he asks, turning to Carmela. "I didn't know you meant it. How could I have known?"

"Cut her loose, and we walk away right now," Damien says. "But if those pictures get out, you'll not only learn how miserable this particular asshat can make your life, but you'll never work anywhere near this business again. Every person who came through this room today knows exactly what kind of man you are."

"That so?" He pushes his chair back and kicks his feet up on the desk. "The way rumors fly in this business, sounds to me like I won't be getting much work after today no matter how this turns out. Seems to me that if I'm getting forced into retirement, I ought to at least walk away with a little nest egg."

He swivels in his chair and looks at Carmela. "No skin off your nose if those pictures are out there, baby. You look gorgeous, and a little sex scandal never hurt anyone in your line of work."

I frown, because those are almost exactly the words Carmela has said to me, and I'm not sure where Bertrand is going with this.

Bertrand points to Damien. "He's the one who doesn't want them released. I say he should pay for that privilege. And we split the money fifty-fifty. Nice little paycheck for you, baby, especially considering the going rate for those pics."

I see a muscle tighten in Carmela's cheek, but then I see something else—a spark of what looks like interest in her eyes. Bertrand sees it too. "Ah! Ah-ha! What did I say? You're a fighter, baby, just like me. A street fighter, who knows when to get in and play dirty."

"I am a fighter, yes," she says, moving closer to him. As she does, she tilts her head and looks straight at me, and my stomach twists into knots. I can't believe I've misjudged her, that I ever backed off my original opinion that she was a narcissistic bitch from hell.

"And you are right," Carmela continues as she reaches across the desk for the folder. "These are quite flattering to me." I expect her to pick up the folder. What she does instead is grab the hotel phone off the desk, then hurl it around so that it smashes into Bertrand's face.

I'm not sure which emotion is stronger—joy that she smashed the asshole's face in, or relief that she wasn't actually considering conspiring with him.

I don't have time to analyze that question, though, because Carmela did the one thing all those self-defense classes for women warn against—she didn't cause enough damage.

Bertrand's nose is bleeding, but that's not enough to stop him, and in almost the same instant that his head bounces back, he lashes out, grabs Carmela by the hair, and starts to slam her face toward the desk—bad enough for any woman, but the next split second could truly destroy Carmela's career.

I hear myself scream—and at the same time, the top of the floor lamp intersects with Bertrand's head, narrowly missing Carmela. He's knocked backward, and in the process lets go of Carmela, who scurries off into a corner.

I'm gasping, unsure what happened, until I see Damien toss the lamp aside even as Ryan vaults the desk and slams Bertrand up against the wall, his grip tight against the vile man's throat as Bertrand continues to struggle, his eyes on Carmela as he screams curses at her.

I realize in that moment that Damien did the only thing he could do to save Carmela from a broken nose—and worse. He was too far away to throw himself in the middle of the fray, and so he snatched up the lamp the second he saw trouble brewing. And with a skill borne of years playing professional tennis, he aimed and swung and hit the rat bastard square on the head, missing Carmela by mere inches in what was undoubtedly an assault on Bertrand calculated down to the last millisecond.

I want to run to him, but right now, his attention is laser-focused on Bertrand. He's only inches from the man, still held in place by Ryan's concrete grip.

"Do not even think of playing hardball with me," Damien says. "You think you know the extent of my resources? Money, power, influence? You don't have a clue how far my reach goes. But I'll tell you this," he adds, getting in even closer, "I damn sure have the resources and connections to bury a worm like you. You want to test me? Release those photos. But be prepared for your world to go to shit if you do. Are we clear?"

Bertrand's mouth opens, but no sound comes out.

"Are we clear?" Damien repeats, and the man nods, looking miserable and just a little sick.

"Let him go," Damien says to Ryan. "Nikki, Carmela. We're leaving."

Carmela has my arm in a vise-grip as we leave the room. We pause in the hallway, and she releases me, then throws her arms around me and then around Damien. "Thank you, Damie. Thank you both."

Damien lets her linger for a moment, then gently extricates himself. He comes to me and folds me into his arms. "You were brilliant," I say.

"Hopefully that's the last of him. He'd be a fool to release those photos now." He kisses me lightly, then brushes his lips across my ear. "Let's go check in with Evelyn and Charles. And then, my darling wife, I want to celebrate our victory."

"That sounds great," I say sincerely, even though I know that he has a completely different type of celebration in mind.

Chapter Ten

D AMIEN'S HAND SLIDES down from my waist to cup my rear as we approach the door to our suite. He tilts my chin up as he bends to brush a kiss over my lips. "Do you know what I want to do now?"

"Tell me," I say, my nipples tightening as I think of his description of how he wanted to take me on the rooftop, and for the first time since I started planning his party, I'm wishing it was some other day.

"I'd rather show you."

I sigh, because what can I say? Obviously what Damien has in mind isn't on the immediate agenda. And I can only hope he'll be pleased by the surprise.

I'm also hoping that everyone is ready inside that room. I'd lingered with Damien in the hall before coming back to the suite, accidentally-on-purpose hitting the button for the lobby when I insisted we take the elevator, then popping into the gift store for some mints. Now, it's been at least ten minutes since we left Bertrand's room, and I'm hoping that's enough time for Carmela and the others to have gotten inside.

I'll know soon enough, I realize, because Damien has his key out and he's swiping the lock. I hear the click, see him push down the handle.

Then the door is opening and we step into the darkened room. I hear Damien's surprised, "hmm," because we never leave the blinds down or the light off, but before he can think too much about it, I reach for the switch.

The room lights up, and at the same time, smiling faces appear from all over the massive living area, a chorus of "Surprise!" ringing out, the word still echoing when Ronnie bolts pellmell toward Damien.

"Were you surprised, Uncle Damie? Were you? Were you?"

"I sure was, Monkey," he says, his expression something I don't usually see on Damien's face as he looks out over the crowd—he looks not only surprised, but humbled.

With a quick grin in my direction, he swings Ronnie up onto his hip, then steps further into the room to greet the dozens of guests who've helped manage to pull this off. Syl and Jackson, Evelyn and Charles, Carmela and Wyatt, Jamie and Ryan. And more. Folks from work like Preston and Lisa and Rachel, new friends like Cass and Siobhan, and Dallas and Jane, and on and on and on.

Soon enough, the guests disperse—some in the living room, some in the kitchen, most going up to the rooftop. I'm heading over to the bar to make drinks for Damien and me, when I see Evelyn pull him into a warm, maternal hug. "Your wife pulled off a doozy."

Damien laughs and swings his arm affectionately around her shoulder as he turns to took at me. "She did. But I know she had help. So thank you."

"Anything for you, kiddo. You know that."

He presses a kiss to her cheek. "Yes," he says, "I do."

I've just handed Damien his drink when Dallas and Jane approach with Noah Carter and Lyle Tarpin. Dallas is one of the investors in The Resort at Cortez, and his scandalous romance with Jane filled the tabloids not that long ago. "Happy birthday, buddy," Dallas says. "We appreciate the invite. Of course, you need to be nice to me if you want to make up for stealing away one of my best men," he adds, glancing at Noah, the tech genius that Damien's been recruiting.

Noah holds up his hands. "What can I say?" he says. "I need more excitement in my life."

The men laugh, and Jane bites back a smile, though I don't get the joke at all. Then again, I've always known there's more to Dallas Sykes than meets the eye.

"How's the movie going?" Damien asks, turning to Jane in what may be a ploy to change the subject.

"Really well," she says, waving at Lyle Tarpin, who sees her and comes over to join us. "Lyle is amazing in it. You and Nikki are coming to the premiere, right?"

"Wouldn't miss it," Damien promises as Jamie comes up beside me and elbows me in the waist.

I turn to her and she cocks her head toward Lyle. I bite back the urge to roll my eyes, then introduce them. "I won't talk business here," Jamie says after they've exchanged pleasantries. She flashes her brightest on-camera smile. "But maybe tomorrow we could schedule an interview?"

Fortunately, Lyle only looks amused as Jamie leads him off toward the bar.

"Ambition in motion," I say to Jane, who laughs.

We chat a bit more, then continue to move through the crowd. Even Edward is here, and Damien pats him on the back jovially when the driver offers his birthday wishes.

Finally, Sylvia and Jackson come over with Ronnie bouncing beside them. "We let her stay up a bit longer than planned. But now she insists on giving you a birthday kiss before Stella takes her up to bed," Sylvia says.

"I think that can be arranged," Damien says, crouching down so that Ronnie can throw her arms around him and plant a big, wet kiss on his cheek.

"I love you, Uncle Damie."

"Love you, too, squirt."

She waves enthusiastically as her dad carries her over to their nanny. And once they're out of sight, Damien pulls me close, his arm around my waist as he looks out over the crowd that fills this enormous room.

"Thank you."

"You already said that," I point out.

"It deserves saying again. Thank you," he repeats, then bends his head to kiss me. "This really is amazing."

And as I look around at this room of colleagues and friends—of people who rearranged plans and came to Santa Barbara on such short notice to help us celebrate—I have to give myself a mental pat on the back, because I agree.

It really is amazing.

"THAT'S EVERYBODY," I say as we shut the door behind Jamie, Ryan, and Wyatt. It's almost two in the morning, which considering we'd started at six, is a sign of remarkable success. Then again, I think the laughter-filled room, the clusters of folks chatting in corners, and the liberal flowing of alcohol were also good indicators.

But there's really only one person whose opinion counts to me. "Did you have a good time tonight?" I ask Damien.

"Did I have a good time?" he repeats. "Come here." He takes my hands and pulls me to him, then closes his mouth hard over mine. He takes a step forward, forcing me against the wall, and I have no time to think as he deepens the kiss. His lips teasing mine, his tongue making me melt.

As his mouth claims me, his hands rise up over the thin knit of my simple sheath dress, moving from my hips to my breasts with the kind of slow, intimate purpose that is making me lose my mind. He cups my breasts roughly, that wildness juxtaposed against a string of sweet kisses that he trails down my neck with such slow and intimate precision that by the time he reaches my collarbone, I am like a wild thing, writhing against him, wanting more and more. Hell, wanting everything.

I slide my hands down to his ass, wanting to pull him closer. But he foils me, taking his hands off my breasts as he bends his mouth lower to bite and suck through the material even as he finds my wrists and lifts my arms above my head, rendering me helpless as he uses his knee to coax my legs apart, then roughly yanking my dress up to my waist.

With one bold move, he rips off my panties, then releases his hold on my wrist long enough to open his fly. He's hard as steel and I'm so damn wet, and as he grabs each of my thighs, I hold onto his shoulders, my back arching as he thrusts hard into me, then takes me hard and fast against the wall, his release coming so quickly I can barely catch my breath.

"Damien," I murmur, but he silences me with a kiss as his hand slips between our joined bodies and he strokes me expertly, making me squirm with a wild, building need that is all the more intense because my feet aren't on the ground, and I'm held up only by the pressure of Damien's body pinning me to the wall.

Higher and higher he takes me, closer and closer, until finally I'm pushed right over the edge and he holds me tight as I explode, my body shattering from the force of the orgasm.

"Thank you for my party," he whispers

when I can breathe again. "I had a very good time."

I laugh, a little trill of victory running through me and I cling to him, enjoying both the moment and the delicious sensation of his body against mine.

"Of course, I've done my part now," I tease. "Tomorrow you have to come up with the evening's entertainment."

"Sweetheart, I think that's already all planned out," he says, tilting his head as if looking up toward the roof.

"Exactly the answer I was hoping for," I admit, making him laugh. "Were you really surprised?"

"Let's just say I had no idea my wife had such a devious side."

I narrow my eyes, because that's not exactly an answer to my question, and I can't help but wonder if he's known all along. I consider asking outright—if I do, I know he'll tell me—but I hold my tongue, too happy with the success of the evening to take even the slightest bit away from all my hard work.

I think about other kinds of hard work as I lead him into the living room and then straddle him on the couch, kissing him lightly before leaning back to grin at him.

"What?" he asks, amusement in his voice.

"I submitted the Dallas proposal early this

morning," I say. "Thank you. For everything."

I see something like pride reflected in his smile. "You're welcome," he says, and I know he understands. I'm not just thanking him for the help he's already given me, but for the support that will come if I get the job.

"There's something else, too," I say, sliding off of him so that I can open one of the drawers on the end table. I reach in and pull out a wrapped box about the size of a book.

His brows rise. "I thought the party was my present."

I shrug. "I wanted to give you something tangible, too. But you're a hard man to shop for." I nod at the present. "Go ahead."

He does, peeling off the paper to reveal a box of Swiss chocolates. He looks up at me, and I see confusion in his eyes. "You got me candy from the confectionary I own?"

"No," I say. "You got them for me. Ages ago, when you took me on the Ferris wheel on the Santa Monica Pier. I saved the box."

He still looks confused, but he opens the box. But there's not chocolate inside, but a variety of small items. He reaches in and lifts out a tiny wrapped bar of soap. It's from Desert Ranch, the exclusive spa that Damien once treated me to. I see his mouth twitch with amusement, his smile growing wider as he pulls out the tiny Eiffel Tower, a miniature bottle with sand from our private beach, and a tiny pine cone from the house in Lake Arrowhead where we'd gone after his trial and recently spent Christmas.

I see the delight on his face as he inspects each item, but when he comes to the last, he laughs outright—the pair of silk panties I'd left in his limo that night we'd met at Evelyn's.

"You're a hard man to shop for," I repeat. "So I took some of my souvenirs and made you a box of memories."

"Nikki, it's…" He trails off, his voice thick with emotion.

"Happy birthday, Mr. Stark. I hope you like it."

"I love it," he says as he pulls me into his arms.

But what I hear is *I love you.*

The End

Don't miss *Anchor Me*,
the fourth book in
The Stark Trilogy!

Check out all of JK's books at
www.jkenner.com

J. Kenner (aka Julie Kenner) is the *New York Times*, *USA Today*, *Publishers Weekly*, *Wall Street Journal* and #1 International bestselling author of over seventy novels, novellas and short stories in a variety of genres.

JK has been praised by *Publishers Weekly* as an author with a "flair for dialogue and eccentric characterizations" and by *RT Bookclub* for having "cornered the market on sinfully attractive, dominant antiheroes and the women who swoon for them." A five-time finalist for Romance Writers of America's prestigious RITA award, JK took home the first RITA trophy awarded in the category of erotic romance in 2014 for her novel, *Claim Me* (book 2 of her Stark Trilogy).

In her previous career as an attorney, JK worked as a lawyer in Southern California and Texas. She currently lives in Central Texas, with her husband, two daughters, and two rather spastic cats.

Visit JK online at www.jkenner.com

Coming Soon From J. Kenner

It's a new chapter in the life of Nikki and Damien Stark ...

Though shadows still haunt us, and ghosts from our past continue to threaten our happiness, my life with Damien is nothing short of perfection. He is my heart and my soul. My past and my future. He is the man who holds me together, and his love fuels my days and enchants my nights.

But when tragedy and challenge from both inside and outside the sanctity of our marriage begin to chip away at our happiness, I am forced to realize that even a perfect life can begin to crack. And if Damien and I are going to win this new battle, it will take all of our strength and love ...

Read on for Chapter One of *Anchor Me* by J. Kenner. Coming April 2017...

Anchor Me

J. Kenner
Unedited preview chapter

Chapter One

I LOOK OUT the window at the beautifully manicured yards that line the wide street down which I am traveling in the sumptuous luxury of a classic Rolls Royce Phantom. A car so sleek and magical that I can't help but feel like a princess in a royal coach.

The road is shaded by parallel rows of massive oaks, their branches arcing over the street toward their counterparts to form a leafy canopy. Morning light fights its way between the leaves, creating golden beams in which dust sparkles and dances as if to a celebratory melody, adding to the illusion that we are moving through a fairy tale world.

All in all, it's a picture perfect moment.

Except it's not. Not really. Or at least not to me.

Because as far as I'm concerned, this is no children's story.

This is Dallas. This is the neighborhood where I grew up. And that means that this isn't a fairy tale. It's a nightmare.

The trees branches aren't stunning—they're grasping. Reaching out to snare me. To hold me tight. To trap me.

The canopy doesn't mark a royal corridor leading to a castle. It leads to a cell. And it's not *The Dance of the Sugarplum Fairies* that fills the air. It is a Requiem for the Dead.

The world outside the car is lined with traps, and if I'm not careful, I'll be sucked in. Destroyed by the darkness that hides behind the false facades of these stately houses. Surrounded not by a bright children's tale but by a horror movie, lured in by the promise of beauty and then trapped forever and slowly destroyed, ripped to pieces by the monsters in the dark.

Breathe, I tell myself. *You can do this. You just have to remember to breathe.*

"Nikki. *Nikki.*"

Damien's voice startles me back to reality, and I jerk upright, as if perfect posture can ward off the ghosts of my memories.

His tone is soft, profoundly gentle, but when I glance toward him, I see that his eyes have dipped to my lap.

For a moment, I'm confused, then I realize that I've inched up my skirt, and my fingertip is slowly tracing the violent scar that mars my inner thigh. A souvenir of the deep, ugly wound that I inflicted upon myself a decade ago when I was desperate to find a way to release all the pent-up anger and fear and pain that swirled inside me like a phalanx of demons.

I yank my hand away, then turn to look out the window, feeling oddly, stupidly ashamed.

He says nothing, but the car moves to the curb and then rolls to a stop. A moment later, Damien's fingers twine with mine. I hold tight, drawing strength, and when I shift to look at him more directly, I see worry etched into the hard angles of that perfect face and reflected in those exceptional eyes.

Worry, yes. But it is the rest of what I see that takes my breath away. Understanding. Support. Respect.

Most of all, I see a love so fierce it has the power to melt me, and I revel in its power to soothe.

He is the biggest miracle of my life, and there are moments when I still can't believe that he is mine.

Damien Stark. My husband, my lover, my best friend. A man who commands an empire with a firm, controlling hand. Who takes orders from no one, and yet today is playing chauffeur so that he can stand beside me while I confront my past.

For a moment, I simply soak him in. His

strength, apparent in both his commanding manner and the long, lean lines of his athletic body. His support, reflected in those dual-colored eyes that see me so intimately. That have, over the years, learned all my secrets.

Damien knows every scar on my body, as well as the story behind each. He knows the depth of my pain, and he knows how far I have come. How far his love has helped me come.

Most of all, he knows what it has cost me to return to Texas. To drive these streets. To look out at this neighborhood so full of pain and dark memories.

With a small shiver, I pull my hand free so that I can hug myself.

"Oh, baby." The concern in his voice is so thick I can almost grab hold of it. "Nikki, you don't have to do this."

"I do." My words sound ragged, my throat too clogged with unshed tears to speak normally.

"Sweetheart—"

I wait, expecting him to continue, but he's gone silent. I see the tension on his face, as if he's uncertain what to say or how to say it—but Damien Stark is never unsure. Not about business. Not about himself. Not about me.

And yet right now he's hesitating. Treating me as if I'm something fragile and breakable.

An unexpected shock of anger cuts through

me. Not at him, but at myself. Because, dammit, he's right. In this moment, I'm as fragile as I've ever been, and that's not a pleasant realization. I've fought so hard to be strong, and with Damien at my side, I've succeeded.

But here I am, all my hard work shot to hell simply because I've returned to my home town.

"You think coming here is a mistake." I snap the words at him, but it's not Damien I'm irritated with, it's me.

"No." He doesn't hesitate, and I take some comfort in the speed and certainty of his response. "But I do wonder if now is the right time. Maybe tomorrow would be better. After your meetings."

We'd come to Texas not so that I could torture myself by driving through my old neighborhood and visiting my estranged mother, but because I'd been invited to submit a proposal to one of the top web development companies in the country. It's looking to roll out a series of apps, both for internal use among its employees and externally for its clients. Only five companies were invited to pitch, and mine is by far the smallest and the the newest. I suspect, of course, that part of the reason I got the invitation is because I'm married to Damien Stark, and because my company has already licensed software to Stark

International.

A year ago, that would have bothered me.

Not anymore. I'm damn good at what I do, and if my last name gets me a foot in the door, then so be it. I don't care how the opportunity comes, because I know that my work is top notch, and if I get the job it will be on the merits of my proposal and my presentation.

It's a huge opportunity, and one I don't want to screw up. Especially since my goal for the next eighteen months is to build up my receivables, hire five employees, and take over the full floor of the building that houses my office condo.

I'd worked on my business plan for months, and I'd been a complete nervous wreck the night I'd handed it to my Master of the Universe, brilliantly entrepreneurial husband for review. When he'd given it the Damien Stark seal of approval, I'd practically collapsed with relief. My plan to grow my business doesn't hinge on me getting this job— but getting it will mean I can bump all my target dates up by six months. More important, winning this contract will put my little company firmly on the competitive map.

My shoulders sag a bit as I meet his eyes. "You're afraid that seeing Mother is going to throw me off my game. That I'll flub tomorrow's meetings, and hurt my chances of landing the contract."

"I want you at your best."

"I know you do," I say sincerely, because Damien has never been anything but supportive. "Don't you get it? That's why we're here. It's like a preemptive strike."

His brow furrows, but before he can ask what I mean, I rush to explain. "Just being in Dallas messes with my head—we both know that. She haunts this town. And before I make my pitch, I need to be certain that I'll be travel back and forth between LA and Dallas without being afraid I'm going to see her around every corner."

The pathetic truth is that lately I've been seeing my mother around all sorts of corners. I've imagined seeing her in Beverly Hills restaurants. On Malibu beaches. In crowded streets. At charity events. I have no idea why this woman I've worked so hard to block from my mind is suddenly at the forefront of my imagination, but she is.

And I really don't want her there.

I draw a breath, hoping he understands. "I need to lay all these demons to rest and just do my work. Please," I add, my voice imploring. "Please tell me you understand."

"I do," he says, then takes my hand and gently kisses my fingertips. As he does, his phone rings. It's sitting on the console, and I can see that the caller is his attorney, Charles Maynard.

"Don't you need to take it?" I ask, as he scowls, then declines the call.

"It can wait."

There's a hard edge to his voice, and I wonder what he's not telling me. Not that Damien keeps me informed about every aspect of his business—considering he pretty much owns and operates the entire planet and a few distant solar systems, that would require far too many updates—but he does tend to keep me in the loop on things that are troubling him.

I frown. It's clear that he's not telling me because I've already got plenty on my mind. And while I appreciate the sentiment, I don't like that—once again—my mother has come between me and my husband.

"You should call him back," I say. "If he's calling on a Sunday it must be important…"

I let the words trail away, hoping to give him an opening, but all he does is shake his head. "Don't worry about it," he says, even as his phone signals an incoming text.

He snatches it up, but not before I see Charles' name flash on the lock screen again, this time with a single word—*Urgent.*

Damien meets my eyes, and for just a moment his frustration is almost comical. Then he snatches up the phone and hits the button to call Charles. A second later, he's saying, "Dammit, I told you I can't be bothered with this right now."

He listens to the response, the furrows in his brow growing deeper. Finally, he sighs, looking more frustrated than I've seen him in a long time.

Cold foreboding washes over me. Damien isn't the kind of man who gets frustrated over business deals. On the contrary, the harder and more challenging the deal, the more he thrives.

Which means this is personal.

"I hear you, Charles, but I'm not paying you for your advice on this. I'm paying you for those resources your PR department is so keen on touting. So use them, dammit. Pull out all the stops and get me some answers by the time I'm back in LA. Fine," he adds after another pause. "Call me if you have something definitive, otherwise I'll see you in a couple of days."

He ends the call and slams the phone back down. I open my mouth, intending to ask him what's happening, but before I get the chance, he pulls me roughly to him and closes his mouth over mine. The kiss is hard, brutal, and I slide closer, losing myself in the wildness. And for this moment at least, I forget my apprehension and his problems. There is nothing but us, our passion a raging blaze that clears away the debris of our lives, stripping us to the bone until there is nothing left but the two of us.

I'm breathing hard when we break apart, my lips bruised and tingling, my body burning. I want to turn around and go back to the hotel. I want to strip off my clothes and feel his hands on me, his cock inside me. I want it wild. Raw. Pain and pleasure so intense I get lost in them. Passion so violent it breaks me. And Damien—always Damien—right there to put me back together again.

I want, but I can't have. Not yet. Because whatever else is going on, I've come to this neighborhood with a purpose, and if I back away now, I may not have the strength to return.

And so as Damien holds me close, I press my cheek against his shoulder and sigh, letting the moment linger. Then I tilt my head up to see his face. Damien doesn't keep secrets from me—not anymore—and I expect him to tell me what the phone call was about. But he says nothing, and my stomach twists miserably. Because I understand Damien well enough to know that the only reason he'll hold back is to protect me. And right now, he's doing his damnedest to protect me from the emotional hell of this trip.

"Damien?"

He clasps his hand around mine, then kisses my fingertips. "I'm sorry. This is our time. Your time. I wouldn't have called back, except—"

"I get it. Really." And I do. I understand why he returned the call. And I understand that this apology is his way of telling me that he's not saying a word about it. Not now. Not until we've seen my mother.

"We should get going," I say.

For a moment, he holds my gaze, as if trying to measure whether I'm truly game-ready. Then he nods and glances down at the phone. "Are you sure you don't want to call her first?"

"No. Let's just go." What I don't say—but I'm sure Damien understands—is that there's a certain amount of appeal in the element of surprise. For once, maybe I'll have the upper hand. And the fact that Damien will be standing on her threshold with me is a bonus. I flash a small but very genuine grin. "I think you intimidate her," I say.

"Me?" His smile is wide and boyish. "I can't imagine why."

"Mmm," I say. "Okay, onward." I gesture regally, indicating he should pull back onto the road. He'd stopped in front of one of the stately homes just a few blocks away from Highland Park Village, one of the ritzier shopping areas in the country, and a place with which I'm very familiar, as I'm pretty sure my mother bought everything from designer diapers to ball gowns for both Ashley and me in the center's boutiques.

But despite the society page sheen of this Dallas enclave, a Phantom stands out. Especially this fully restored beauty.

"The neighbors are jealous," I say, nodding toward two women openly gawking at the car as they jog. "They're wondering who's moving into the neighborhood with more money than they have."

Damien brushes off the comment. "It's not the price that intrigues them," he says. "It's the beauty. The craftsmanship. The restoration. This is a neighborhood that thrives on appearances," he adds, nodding to his right and the line of elegant homes we are passing. Then he glances to his left, his eyes roaming slowly over me. "And this car—and the woman in it—are two things of pure beauty."

My cheeks warm. "I'll agree with you on the car," I say modestly, though I can't deny that the compliment pleases me. "But I think they're mostly fascinated with the man behind the wheel—and the fact that he's on the right side of the car."

It's odd being on the driver's side and not doing the driving, but this 1967 Phantom V limo is as British as they come, having once been a formal British royal family touring limousine.

No wonder I feel like a fairy tale princess.

We'd come to Dallas for my work, but when Damien had learned about the trip, he'd made an appointment to see a retired aerospace engineer he'd once met at a classic car show whose hobby-turned-second-career is restoring Bentleys and Rolls Royces to mint condition. We'd gone straight to his home in North Dallas after arriving, and Damien had spent two hours in a state of bliss talking about this Phantom.

"How much?" Damien had asked, after he'd inspected the limo throughly, commenting on the brilliant design and mechanical prowess with the kind of rapture with which most people speak of movie stars. I couldn't deny that he was right about the car's beauty and uniqueness. It's painted a typical black, but the sheen is such that every angle and curve is set off to perfect advantage. And the interior is as elegant as a palace, the wood carved and polished to perfection, the leather seats soft and supple. The car is rare, too, as apparently only five hundred and sixteen of this particular model were made.

The engineer quoted a six-figure price, and Damien pulled out his checkbook without the slightest hesitation. Less than an hour later, we were driving down the North Dallas Tollroad in the latest addition to Damien's vehicular menagerie, and Damien's giddy expression reminded me of a little boy on Christmas morning.

Now, he maneuvers the limo through Highland Park, the well-heeled neighborhood in which I grew up. Though my family's net worth never came close to Damien's, we were hardly scraping by. My grandfather had made a fortune in oil, and though much of that was lost in the recession—and later by my mother's bad management—there's no denying that I was a child of privilege, just like every other kid living in these massive, tony mansions.

I'd walked away from all that when I'd moved to Los Angeles, intent on escaping my past. I'd wanted a new life, a new Nikki. And I'd been determined to make it on my own without my mother's baggage holding me down.

Now, I can't help but smile as I look at Damien. At this car that cost more than most people earn in a year. It's funny how things shift. I was wealthy in Dallas, but miserable. Now I'm filthy rich in Los Angeles, and happier than I could ever have imagined. Not because of the bank account, but because of the man.

"You're smiling," he says, sounding pleased, and I'm once again struck by the fact that he is as much on pins and needles as I am. Damien, however, isn't worried about seeing my mother. Damien is worried about me.

"I was just thinking how happy I am," I admit, and then tell him why.

"Because the money isn't the heart of what we are to each other," he says. "You'd love me even if I was destitute."

"I would," I admit, then flash an impish smile. "But I can't deny that I like the perks." I run my hand over the dashboard. "Of course, I'd like *this* particular perk better if Edward were here."

"Not satisfied with just holding my hand, Mrs. Stark?"

Usually when we're in a limo, Damien's personal driver, Edward, acts as chauffeur. But Edward's not with us on this trip, and even if he were, I know Damien would insist on driving his new toy.

"I'm fine with hand holding for now," I say archly. "But later, I want more. Later, I want your hands on all of me."

The glance he shoots me overflows with heat and promise. "I think that can be arranged."

"Eyes on the road, driver," I say, then point. "And turn here."

He does, and immediately my mood downshifts again. Because now we're on my actual street. Now, we're a few blocks away from my childhood home.

I draw a breath. "Almost there. And I'm fine," I add before he has a chance to ask. I'm not fine—not entirely—but I'm hoping that by saying it I'll banish the hideous aching in my gut and the nausea that is starting to rise up inside me.

"Just tell me when."

I nod, and for a moment I picture us driving past, just going on and on until we're out of the neighborhood, back in Dallas proper and far, far away from the memories that are now washing over me like wave after wave crashing onto a sandy shore. Me locked in a pitch black room because little girls need their beauty sleep, and my sister Ashley whispering to me through the closed door, promising me that nothing is lurking in the dark to hurt me. A stylist tugging and pulling on my long golden hair, ignoring my tears and cries of pain as my mother stands by, telling me to control myself. That I'm embarrassing her. My mother gripping my arm as she tugs me up the walkway to register for my first pageant, my eyes still red from the sting of her hand on my kindergarten-age bottom, a reminder that beauty queens don't complain and whine.

I think of a dinner plate with the tiniest portion of plain chicken and steamed vegetables while my mother and sister eat cheesy lasagna, and my mother telling me that if I want to be a pageant winner, I need to watch every calorie and think of carbohydrates as the devil. Then her mouth pursing in disapproval when I insist that I don't care about being a pageant winner. That I just want to not be hungry.

I was never good enough. Too chunky, too slouchy, too lackluster. Even with an array of crowns and titles, I never met her expectations, and I don't remember a time when she ever felt like mother or friend. Instead, she was the strict governess of stories. The wicked step-mother. The witch in the gingerbread house.

My older sister Ashley escaped her clutches by the simple act of not winning the pageants in which she entered. After several failures, my mother gave up. And though I tried to fail, too, I was cursed with crowns and titles.

For years, I'd thought that Ashley'd had the better end of the deal. It was only later, when she killed herself after her husband left her, that I understood how deep Ashley's scars had run, too. Mine were physical, the self-inflicted scars of a girl who took a blade to her own skin, first to release the pressure and gain some control, then later to mar my pageant-perfect legs and end the madness of that horrific roller-coaster.

Ashley's were under the surface, but still deep. And at the core, both mine and my sister's scars were inflicted by our mother.

My heart races, and I force myself to breathe steadily. To calm down. We're almost there, and if I'm going to see my mother, I need to be in control. Show even the slightest weakness, and she'll pounce on it.

And, yes, I've grabbed the upper hand before—I sent her back to Texas after she tried to take over planning my wedding, ignoring what I wanted in favor of her own skewed vision—but in Dallas she definitely has the home court advantage.

"Nine-three-seven?" Damien asks, referring to the address, and I nod.

"The first house on the left after the bend," I say, and I'm proud of how normal my voice sounds. I can do this. More than that, I want to do it. Clear the air. Wash away all the cobwebs.

Basically, I'm doing the parental equivalent of burning sage in a house tainted with bad memories.

The thought amuses me, and I'm about to tell Damien when the car rounds the bend and my humor fades.

Moments later, my childhood home comes into view. But it's not my mother's Cadillac parked in the drive. Instead, I'm staring at two unfamiliar Land Rovers, a Mercedes convertible, and a moving van.

So where the hell is my mother?

60352540R00085

Made in the USA
Lexington, KY
03 February 2017